Daisy An
Dac

Janey Clarke

Janey Clarke

First Published in 2022 by Blossom Spring Publishing
Daisy and the Dazzling Dachshunds
Copyright © 2022 Janey Clarke
ISBN 978-1-7397357-5-3
E: admin@blossomspringpublishing.com
W: www.blossomspringpublishing.com
Published in the United Kingdom. All rights reserved under
International Copyright Law. Contents and/or cover may not
be reproduced in whole or in part
without the express written consent of the publisher.
Names, characters, places and incidents are either
products of the author's imagination
or are used fictitiously.

CHAPTER ONE

"Daisy! Daisy! We need a pet basket now! Help us Daisy! Hurry!"

My doorbell rang again and again. Loud knocking, accompanied by the shouts had made me jump. My paintbrush fell onto my paper, landing with a splosh onto my sunflower painting. I jumped to my feet and raced downstairs from my study. As fast as my elderly legs could go! I'd been living in my converted stable cottage for some weeks. The Priory House, dominated a central courtyard, having stable wings either side of the courtyard in the shape of a U. One side of the stables had been converted into cottages, in one of which I lived. The opposite side was still in disrepair. My study, a small upstairs bedroom, had fantastic views over Bodmin Moor. Since my move to the Priory, I'd resumed my botanical painting.

"What is it? What's all the noise?" I asked as I flung open my front door.

"Daisy! Help us! We need a pet basket for these. They need a vet at once!" Sheila, an octogenarian who lived in one of the two refurbished apartments in Priory House, stood on my doorstep, with her grandchildren, eight year old Rosie, and ten year old Ben.

"We found them on our walk and they are going to die," wailed Rosie.

"I bet they're from that puppy farm," said

ten-year-old Ben. He clutched a tiny scrap of fluff, his anxious freckled face peering down at it.

"She's escaped with her babies," said Rosie, cuddling another tiny pup.

"Hurry Daisy, we must get them to the vet," insisted Sheila. Her white helmet of curly hair bent over the small King Charles Cavalier dog in her arms. Brown liquid eyes stared up me through dirty matted fur. Anxious and sad, the eyes were pleading. I felt such a rise of fury at the cruelty of the puppy farmer that it overwhelmed me.

"Come in, I'll get the basket." Listless, without any flicker of emotion, the dog and her pups were placed on a soft, clean fleece, in the basket. The dog sniffed at it, as if unused to such cleanliness or luxury. The dog basket was used for Flora, on outings and puppy training classes. Another cottage resident, Inspector Tenby, our local police Inspector had taken over his daughter's puppy when she went to Dubai. A boisterous fluffy little mongrel who was adorable. Flora and my cat Cleo had bonded and become best friends. They decided between them that Flora would come to live with me!

"I'll come with you," began Sheila, rising awkwardly from her chair. Sheila was disabled with arthritis. I realised that her morning walk had been her day's limit.

"No, Sheila. I'll take the dogs to the vet. Can you look after Cleo and Flora, and take them into the garden? And text the others," I added.

Ben helped me carry the cage. "Take Ben with you, he can help," called Sheila from my doorway.

"Okay Ben, you're coming with me to the vets." I smiled at him and waved to Sheila and Rosie.

"Daisy, I love your van, and the words 'BURT'S BEEFY BANGERS' on the side of it. That huge smiling face of Burt holding a large sausage on a fork is great! Everyone at my school knows your van. I tell everyone you're my friend." Ben helped put the cage in the back of my van. He patted Burt's large smiling face, and the large sausage on its fork on the side of my van, as he walked round.

"Wow!" was all he said.

Ben jumped into the passenger seat, fastened his seatbelt, and grinned at me. "Nan says you lot caught a murderer, and the Templar Creeper last month." Ben said as we drove off.

"Yes, we helped the police." I replied.

"Nan said you lot are now called the Priory Five. She says you're going into business as private investigators."

"She said what?" I shrieked. The van jumped in shock. Sheila, Ben's grandmother was an ardent fan of American T.V. crime shows. Sheila lived in a refurbished apartment, as did Maggie, fortyish with curly black and a cheerful smile, our resident housekeeper in the old Priory House. Jim a retired civil servant, tall white-haired with a charismatic personality, and Martin a former academic, who sported a wispy beard and straggly ponytail, lived as did Tenby, a police inspector, alongside me in the other cottages. We were five people who had helped Tenby catch a murderer a few weeks ago, so Sheila had nicknamed us the Priory Five.

"Nan said you found a dead body in your cottage. On your first night wasn't it? She was stabbed with a dagger, wasn't she?" I opened my mouth to answer. It was a waste of time. Ben, just like his Nan, loved to talk. "I love my Nan living here. Her house got too big for her to look after. She lives in an apartment now in the Priory House. It's very old, like something out of a museum."

"Yes, it's very old, some of the ruins, and the old kitchen date from Norman times," I replied. The Priory kitchen overlooked the courtyard facing down that U shape. A vast room, it had a raised area with stone arches of considerable antiquity and was mentioned in the Domesday book. The Priory kitchen was the hub of the house. A huge refectory table, left over since the monk's ownership of the Priory, contrasted with a huge scarlet Aga and kitchen cupboards of vivid scarlet lacquer. But it was a welcoming and comfortable room, despite the antiquity and vast area.

"Nan gives us cookies and coke beside the old arches in the kitchen. It's like Hogwarts."

The road wound through the Cornish

countryside. Bleak moorland gave way to small green fields and wooded areas, enclosed in stone walls. A stream, swollen with melting snows, rushed alongside the road. I took my time through the narrow lanes. They twisted and turned, and zigzag bends came suddenly upon the unwary driver. Locals raced around, knowing every inch of the lanes, delighting in the lack of tourists clogging the roads. The fresh green growth slowly appearing in the hedgerows gave a welcome sign of spring which buoyed my spirits.

"Your cottage was an old stable wasn't it?"

"Yes Ben, four cottages were converted from one side of the stable courtyard," I said.

"I love going out the archway from the stable courtyard! I'll bet it had huge gates to keep out invaders. We live in a straight road, it's boring." The journey passed with school activities, games, and football chat. Perhaps I'd have been better taking Rosie. She didn't look quite so chatty.

The vets car park was already crowded. I groaned, expecting a long wait with my already stressed passengers. A figure dressed in scrubs, dashed around the corner towards us. He pointed at my van.

"You must be Daisy." I got out of the van. He gave me a sharp look and grinned. "Definitely Daisy!" he said, eyeing my purple streaked hair, and vivid purple and pink embroidered jacket. My new life in Cornwall had included an image change. No more boring clothes and dull colours. My colourful new haircut cried out for the zingiest colours and clothes I could find. "I'm the vet. Jim rang to say you were on your way, and the waiting room would be too traumatic for them." Ben rushed to the back doors of the van and opened them. He reached for one side of the cage and the vet went to the other. "Oh, good grief! You poor little things. Let's get you sorted."

The two of them carried the cage through a back door, and into a small room. The antiseptic smell was overpowering and reassuring at the same time. Gently, the mother and pups were placed on the table.

"What about the RSPCA? Can't they stop the puppy farming?" I asked, turning towards the young vet, his eyes intent as he examined the dogs. His face darkened with anger, as he began to cut lumps of tangled fur from the mother.

"They go up to his land, but never find any signs of a puppy farm," he answered. "Same with the police. We know it's there. I live near that valley, and sometimes I can hear the dogs barking at night. He's got it well hidden, somewhere in the hills, or in an old quarry. We think it's owned by a newcomer called Davies. No proof of course. I get an endless stream of puppies, all malnourished and neglected. Some even have life-threatening illnesses. I feel sorry for the new owners. So much money spent out with such hope, and then heartbreak, especially for the children." He was such a young man to be disillusioned so early in his career by the cruelty inflicted on animals.

All I could do was nod sympathetically and help place the puppies back in the basket.

"I'll pay for the bills now with my credit card. Martin is the new owner of the Priory. He'll settle all bills in the future. Can we take them home with us? We have lots of room there, and there's plenty of people to look after them."

"I'll help look after them!" Ben assured the vet.

"I think you can foster them for the moment. There's no room here for them. The official paperwork can be done later."

Ben and I emerged carrying the cage. All three dogs had been checked. We returned with special food, medicine, and detailed instructions. The journey back was full of Ben's chatter. All went well. Actually, I let his voice drift over me, until the questions began.

"Jim is the tall guy with the limp. Nan says he used to be a spy. Was it MI6? Was he like James Bond?" That I passed over with some remark. "I love your van. Why have you got it? Why did you move here?"

How to explain to a ten-year-old? If I'd been decades younger I could have claimed a midlife crisis. I didn't want to tell him about my marital breakup, and subsequent divorce, and the sale of the family house. I didn't want to tell him that I was terrified of my approaching big birthday. The unexpected arrival of Cleo my rescue cat just before I moved, the intriguing information about my birth in Cornwall, (I was adopted) all led to my mad impulse to rent a Cornish cottage in the Priory on Bodmin Moor.

"My son's friend has a garage and sold me the van at a bargain price. I sold my house and decided to move to Cornwall. That's why I'm here Ben." The journey continued with Ben's chatter, questions, and constant twisting around to check the dogs. Without a murmur they had accepted the vets handling. In fact, I thought they were too listless. The vet told me that food, rest, and company would effect a dramatic change.

We drew into the courtyard. Rosie had obviously been on the lookout from my lounge window, she rushed out with Sheila following. The Priory kitchen overlooked the courtyard and Jim, Maggie and Martin had also been watching for us. The cage was taken into the Priory kitchen, everyone following, eager to see the new arrivals.

On our arrival at the Priory kitchen, Ben waved the vets list of instructions under Martin's nose.

"The vet cut the worst of the matted hair off them. We have to bath them and try to get the rest of the tangles out." Everyone had looked at the pups and their mother from a distance, taking care not to frighten them with too many faces.

"The back kitchen in the Priory is ideal. There's a huge sink there, and I'll bring towels." Maggie said to Martin. "Then we can get them washed and brushed." Ben and Rosie dashed into the back kitchen, at the ready to help with the puppies.

I backed slowly out of the doorway.

"Not going to help?" whispered Jim behind me.

"No thank you! I got lumbered with Flora a couple of weeks ago. And I'd already got a rescue cat! No more puppies for me, thank you very much, I've done my bit," I said.

"Come on then. Let's look at the O.S. maps that are in the library, and the old maps of mine workings and quarries in that area. There are even old rent books that may have information. That man must have that puppy farm well hidden. Let's see if we can find it," said Jim.

"Why? Why are we looking?" I said, eyeing him suspiciously.

Sheila's voice echoed down the corridor towards us. "Why? Surely you don't need to ask. We're going to find that puppy farm, and we're going to put the owner out of business, and preferably in jail! The Priory Five is going to investigate!"

CHAPTER TWO

I followed Jim into the library. Sheila joined the others with the pups in the back kitchen. Jim went to a bookshelf. He selected maps, and several old estate rent books.

"These may provide information, lost to the present-day maps," he said. I nodded and walked over to the long window. As I looked out across the terrace and lawn, to the moorland stretching out to the horizon, my thoughts were elsewhere. Another investigation was not on my 'to do' list. Sheila and Jim were both eager to begin. But I'd not forgotten the terror and fear that I felt when faced with the masked gunman, and Jim had been shot. Jim still limped from the bullet wound he got in his leg. There had been a burglary, an arson attack, a murder, and shootout! I didn't want to face all that sort of stuff again. For goodness sake! We were no longer full of youthful vigour. We were full of pills and potions for our age-related aches and pains.

"You don't want to do it again, do you?" Jim said, from behind the maps and books piled in front of him.

"No, I don't. Have you forgotten you were shot at?" I said and turned and faced him.

"I'm not likely to forget, when our gunman keeps sending you postcards!" he retorted.

"I don't want to think about him, let alone receive post from him!" I threw my hands up in the air. I'd bested our gunman a few times, using hairspray, amongst other bizarre weapons that had been handy. The gunman had liked my innovative use of objects as weapons. After he escaped abroad, he sent me the occasional postcard. "No, I don't want to get involved in any more gunfights or attacks."

Jim raised his hand, in warning. "Don't you dare say at our age, or you'll get aggro from me. Do you really want to do nothing?" He stared at me intently. "You took the dogs to the vet. You know the state they were in. Fed and watered, but starved of human company and love, and in a cage for their whole lives!"

"Okay, okay. I can't stand by, but surely the police and the RSPCA are the ones..."

The voice came from the open doorway, I don't know how long he'd been standing there, but Inspector John Tenby strode in, a new resident in one of the Priory refurbished stable cottages. There had been a murder in that cottage. No one else would live there, and he jumped at the chance of joining us in the beautiful surroundings of the Priory. Tenby had obviously heard our conversation.

"Normally I'd say, speaking as a policeman, keep out of our business. But we can't find out where he's keeping the dogs. If you could find that out, then leave the rest to us, that would work."

Jim smiled at Tenby, then looked at me. "Sure, we can do that, can't we Daisy?"

I knew when I was beaten, but I hated that smug look on Jim's face. "Yes, okay, we'll see if we can find the puppy farm."

"Great. Then you must leave it to us to deal with the guys at the farm. Must dash, burglary to deal with," said Tenby.

"See, we've even got police permission to investigate. We find the location of the puppy farm and then we call Tenby," said Jim. I just nodded. That smile on Jim's face spelt trouble. Yes, we'd investigate and find the location. But I knew Jim would charge in to rescue the dogs. He'd have a gun in his waistband, and his ankle holster was always ready primed for action. Sheila would wield a cane in one hand and a shotgun in the other. I closed my eyes. Perhaps, just perhaps, this investigation would only be a question of us finding the actual puppy farm. Sitting down at the table, and picking up an ancient map and magnifying glass, I sighed. Who was I kidding? There was going to be another shootout, chase, and involvement with bad guys.

Was that shiver up my spine of fear, or excitement?

"At least, this investigation starts without a murdered woman," I said.

"Yet!" was Jim's reply, "not yet!"

"Hello Daisy," the hesitant voice of Gerald Higgins, crept around the door. Gerald and his huge glasses followed the voice. He was blinking and smiling nervously at me. An owl, that's what Gerald always reminded me of. I was aware of Jim's scrutiny as he watched for my reaction. It was the first time we'd spoken since the Templar Creeper debacle. Gerald had 'given help and aid to the enemy' as Sheila had said.

"Hi Gerald, perhaps you can be of help to us," I said. Those last weeks were horrifying and frightening, but they were in the past. Time to move forward and make my peace with Gerald. I'll swear both men heaved sighs of relief. What had they expected me to do? Let's not go there, I thought. "Do you know anything about this puppy farm guy?" I said.

"Yes, it's Hilltop farm, and been in the hands of the Davies family for generations. Old man Davies lived there and leased all the land out to other farmers when he became too old to work it." Gerald delved into the satchel he always carried with him. A map was brought out. Copied from an O.S. map, it was personalised with lots of highlighted additional information.

"Here's the Davies farm," Gerald pointed on the map. "It's not far from here, but a lot further up on top of the moor. It's bleak and wild up there, with stretches of open moorland and rocky outcrops and close to the Smugglers Way."

"The Smugglers Way?" I asked. "I've never heard of that."

"Based loosely on a traditional route across the moor, it links the harbours of Boscastle on the Atlantic coast, and Looe on the English Channel. It's now a walk for hikers. There are tourist maps and guides on it now," said Jim.

"Old man Davies died a couple of years ago. A distant cousin inherited the farm, moved in, and this new Davies has let it go to rack and ruin. Keeps mainly to..." began Gerald.

"...Himself! Nasty bit of work that chap is. Don't bother with any of us locals, so we don't bother with the likes of him," interrupted Demelza from the doorway. Our official deputy housekeeper, as she liked to be called, Demelza Trethowan stood there. Black hair hung down her back in long tresses but her striking good looks were marred by a zigzag scar running down one cheek. Always she dressed in black, usually with black lace somewhere on a skirt, blouse, or scarf. A tray was held in her hands. "Two coffees and a tea," she brought it across to the desk and plonked it down.

"Demelza, you always make tea just how I like it," I sighed with pleasure, cradling the hot mug in my hands.

"Of course, I do. Everyone gets what they like, but yours is special." Turning to Gerald, she said, "Daisy's my cousin, we're family." She flounced out of the door, her long skirts swishing as she walked. The white wellington boots she always wore gave a strange slurping sound on the polished wood floor.

At Gerald's look of enquiry, Jim laughed, "she's told Daisy, ever since she arrived, that she's family. Daisy keeps telling her that she has no Cornish relations," Jim chuckled as he reached for his coffee. It was as well he was concentrating on his coffee and hadn't seen my face. Now, it was quite possible that Demelza had been right all along! I thought of the envelope that had arrived a few days ago, and the accompanying note and birth certificate it had contained. "Carry on Gerald, you were telling us about the farm," prompted Jim.

"Well, this guy keeps himself close to the farm. Shops in Bodmin once a week at the supermarket. Has a few chickens about the place, and a few sheep. Every Saturday, he drinks in the pub, sits in the corner, speaks to nobody, and staggers home drunk. There's a lot of talk in the village, about strange vans delivering stuff. No one knows what that's all about."

"Why is he suspected of being the puppy farmer?" I asked.

"He's always flush with money, can pay for whisky Saturday night, and not the cheap stuff! Even wears a Rolex and has a top of the range Jaguar car." Gerald said, delighted to be of help to us. His owl like face creased with pleasure.

"Alice, that widow woman, who works for Davies at Hilltop farm, has been found dead!" Maggie burst into the room, almost shouting at us in her excitement and distress.

"Murdered?" was Jim's query.

"They say she slipped on the path on her way home. She hit her head on a rock and drowned in the river."

"But it's not very deep there, surely not enough for anyone to drown in," said Martin, who had followed Maggie into the room.

"Suspicious," was Jim's comment. He stood

up and turned to face me. "That's your fault! Looks like you got your murdered woman, after all Daisy! You've got your dead body!"

CHAPTER THREE

"Tenby won't want us to investigate the puppy farm now. Not when there's been a murder," began Martin. Always nervous of authority, he worried endlessly about *'doing the right thing.'* And Tenby will never tell us police business," he added.

"He might!" boomed Tenby's voice. He walked into the library. A large man, he had a burly cheerful looking exterior. But his hard cold eyes could focus like a laser when on police business. Hugo the former owner, had offered him the cottage that had lain empty since a woman had been murdered in it. Tenby, whose landlord had a buyer for his flat, jumped at the chance of joining us in the Priory. His daughter had been offered an exciting job in Dubai and had asked him to look after her puppy. Flora the puppy, and my cat Cleo had become friends, and both insisted that Flora should move in with me!

"He might think you lot might help him." The large policeman had investigated the murder in the cottage. We had 'helped' or impeded that investigation. Originally the Priory House had been intended as a boutique hotel with luxury holiday cottages, however the money had dried up. After the murder, Hugo the former owner sold everything to Martin, a thirty something geek, who had moved into one of the cottages. Martin had made a fortune in Bitcoins. He had offered Sheila, the disabled octogenarian, Jim a retired civil servant, and me ninety-nine year leases for a peppercorn rent. The last couple of months had caused this varied assortment of folk from different backgrounds and ages, to gel together into a close-knit group.

All eyes swivelled towards the policeman. His usual jovial features were set in a hard mask. The eyes were a steel grey, and very angry.

"She was murdered all right. Still waiting for the autopsy for all the facts. But it's obvious to me."

"Oh no! She was such a sweet little woman. She'd help anybody. Why she stayed working for that Davies man, I just don't know," said Maggie.

"I do, he paid her nearly double the going rate. No one else would work for him, she got paid well. That's what the neighbour told me," said Tenby.

"Why are you giving us this information?" said Jim, a wary look creeping across his face.

"Yes, why? You usually tell us to keep our noses out of your police business," I added.

Tenby leant against the doorway, and obviously took time to consider his words. "This isn't straightforward police business. It's nasty, and evil in a furtive manner. No one, and there's been plenty that has tried over the years, no one, has ever got anything on this guy. You lot, with your gabby innocent senior citizen act, can find out things that a policeman can't." He stepped forward into the room. "But this is murder! Things have taken a vicious turn here. I'm not sure if this murder is connected to the puppy farm or Davies. It may be a coincidence. I don't like coincidences. Don't believe in them. Snoop around, but for goodness sake, watch your backs!" Abruptly, he turned and left the room. There was a silence as each of us considered his words.

"It's all your fault, Daisy. You practically wished a dead body upon us!" Jim said. His words fell into the silence. All eyes turned towards me. At my startled and furious expression, Jim started to laugh.

"It's no laughing matter! Some poor woman is dead. Why? And who killed her? How are we going to find out about it if you turn it into a joke!" I said, furious at his words. I put my hands on my hips and glared at him.

"Sorry," Jim held up one hand in mock surrender, as he tried to swallow a laugh.

"Last time we went investigating, we snooped around the village. Let's do that! We found out lots of *'Intel',*" Sheila said, eager to change the subject. Our octogenarian was a keen follower of trending fashions and spent her wakeful night hours following American T.V. cop shows.

"Intel? You've been watching those American cop shows again," said Maggie, a fond smile on her face for the older woman. "Davies goes to the pub on Saturday night, that's about his only outing, except for his weekly supermarket shop," added Maggie.

"What about Alice's activities? Is there

anything we can follow up there?" said Maggie.

Jim reached into his desk drawer. He brought out a fresh notebook. The library was a large room with floor length windows that overlooked the terrace, lawns, and Bodmin Moor in the distance. Wood panelled walls were interspersed with bookcases crammed with books. A former owner had obviously been a bibliophile. The fireplace was vast and held huge logs which heated the entire room, giving off a welcome warmth on a cold spring day. Squashy leather armchairs, a couple of sofas, and the occasional tables dotted about the room had large pottery lamps lit against the dreary gloomy morning. Martin and Jim both had a large desk each in the library. A table stood before one of the tall windows now covered with Gerald's maps and pamphlets. During our last investigation, Jim had written copious notes on everything we did, everywhere we went, and all our conversations with people of interest. This seemed to be a sign, a beginning of our next episode of mayhem and murder. I sighed and glanced around.

All my fellow residents had now congregated in the library. Maggie sat on the other side of Jim's desk, her eyes bright with anticipation. Martin sat at his larger desk, all his computers were closed down, which was a first for Martin. His attention was entirely focused on Jim, on that notebook, and Jim's pen that was travelling at speed across the pristine pages.

Sheila, in the armchair, bent forward, her knitting completely forgotten. One needle was clutched in her hand, the other needle, stitches slipping off one by one, hung over the arm of her chair. Her mouth was open, and she nodded her curly white head in excitement. I sat in my usual armchair, between the fire and the window. It was warm, and I had an uninterrupted view of Bodmin Moor. Unable to quell my interest, I finally joined in the conversation and excitement of the others.

"Alice belonged to a knitting group. Sheila could attend that, chat to the others in the group, and see what she could pick up there," suggested Maggie.

"Perhaps my stitches!" laughed Sheila as she retrieved her fallen knitting and began to set it to rights.

"Where did you find the dogs, Sheila?" I asked and stood up, walking over to the map spread out on the desk.

Lifting the stitch free needle, Sheila stretched out and pointed to a spot. It wasn't far from the Priory, which was why Sheila had made it a frequent walk on her good days.

"Here, just beside the path, it's almost as if they were hidden under a bush," she said.

"And Tenby said Alice was found here in this stream, is that right?" I asked Jim.

"Yes, some distance away and beneath the same footpath. That can't be a coincidence. Alice worked for Davies. Now she's dead and those dogs we found were on that very same footpath."

"Let's check out that path, keeping well away from the crime scene. There may be clues near to where Sheila found the dogs," Jim said and rose to his feet. "But nowhere near the crime scene!" he repeated.

"Can you return today, or will it be too much for you?" I asked Sheila.

"It will be too much for me to walk twice in one day, but I can show you on the map." Again, the knitting needle pointed to a rocky outcrop beside the path. "Use that rock as your guide, I found them just before it," she said.

"I'll come," I said, walking towards the library door, to join Martin and Jim.

"I've work to do in the kitchen, so the dogs can come in with me," said Maggie. "It's warm, and they will probably spend most of their time in there, so they may as well get used to it. And they are very sleepy, so should be no bother."

Sheila sat silently, her face now miserable. I nudged Jim and nodded my head towards her. He nodded back at me.

"Sheila you're great on the Internet. Do you mind doing some research for us? Delivery of dog supplies to this area, possible sales of puppies from the farm, all that sort of thing. I think it's a possibly useless task I'm giving you, but it could give us valuable leads if you find anything."

"Okay Jim, I'll get on it right away!" Sheila brightened immediately, and her enthusiasm swept away the depression at her disability.

Sheila suffered arthritis and had good days when she could use a stick to walk, and bad days when she needed a wheelchair.

"Use my computer," said Martin, and switched on one of his new ones.

"Can I really Martin?" Sheila gasped. "That's great, so much bigger and easier than my iPad."

As we walked across the cobbled courtyard, I said to the two men beside me. "That was well done, both of you. Sheila was..."

"Okay, okay," both men cut me off in mid-sentence. Their embarrassment was obvious. I smiled to myself. They were both really good guys.

It was cold, wet, and windy. That morning had a dreary feel of a winter's day, which promised even more rain and gales by nightfall. I knew it couldn't be far to go, Sheila's walking range was very limited. We trudged on, hoping we would get back before the storm.

"That path leads down to the village and Alice's cottage. This was her walk from Hilltop farm to her home," Jim said as we reached a fork in the path. The rocky walls turned into high banks, the trees arched overhead, and we were suddenly walking into a leafy tunnel. Walking on upwards, the path opened out into a clearing and then we emerged onto the moor itself.

"There's the rock ahead of us, and here's

some bushes." Martin cried out in excitement and rushed towards them.

"Where did Alice...?" I paused. How did I finish that sentence? Had she been murdered as Tenby thought. Or had it been an unfortunate accident?

"Look, over there, that must be the crime scene," Jim said.

Along the valley bottom, we could see figures in hi vis jackets moving around. The path we were on led around, and above the figures below.

"There's nothing here that could be connected with that crime scene. Is there? Don't want Tenby mad at us." Martin's face showed his worry at that possibility.

"No, if we concentrate around the rocks and along this part of the footpath, we are well away from those guys," Jim said.

It was Martin who found it. Under some bushes, there was a flattened patch of grass. "The dogs must have been here! There's a piece of white fur caught in these brambles."

Jim bent down, with difficulty. That gunshot wound of a few weeks ago was still causing him trouble. He'd been furious with the doctors when he complained of his slow healing. He had stormed into the kitchen at the Priory. "Damn the doctor, said what did I expect at my age!" I hid a smile at the memory and began searching behind the bushes.

Martin had walked further along the path. "Here is a piece of blanket, and it's got fur on it. The dogs didn't escape. They were brought here! Alice must have brought them." He lifted the dirty blanket, and a scrap of paper fell at his feet.

CHAPTER FOUR

"It's a list, obviously scribbled in haste." Jim pulled out a plastic bag from one of his many pockets and dropped in both items. Sealing the bag, he held it in his hands for a moment, and then looked at me. Hopefully!

"Okay," I said, and sighing, took it from him and put in my shoulder bag. After more fruitless minutes searching, we grew cold and tired. My hands were frozen despite the mitts I wore. My scarf wrapped round my neck was bright orange and glowed in harmony with my mitts. But both were no protection against the cutting bite of the north wind. We could see the men still working on their search around the crime scene. It was getting even colder, and the wind now had a definite chill factor, as it swept along the ridge eddying around us.

"There's nothing more to find here. Let's go home. We've proved that someone took the dogs and hid them. It all points to Alice. We know she worked there, and this is on her route home," said Jim.

"Do you think that's why she was murdered? Do you think it's because she took those three dogs?" Martin said, as we walked down the path. The scrubby bushes were like skeletons without their leaves. The moorland could be dispiriting and gloomy in the approaching twilight. That walk back to the Priory was to get out of the cold, but also to get into the light and warmth of the Priory. As night closed in, the brooding moor had a presence, an evil presence which drove us onward.

"Could be, in fact Martin I think that's the most likely scenario," said Jim.

"That list might be the real reason. Surely, the loss of two pups and a dog, wouldn't be important enough for a puppy farmer to murder someone?" I argued.

"It could be the list," Jim replied. "The sooner we get home and try to understand this list the better," Jim said, walking faster, despite his limp getting more pronounced.

We had reached the courtyard when Maggie rushed towards us.

"I was going to text you but saw you from the window. I've got Flora ready. Martin there's a puppy training class available in half an hour. A beginner's class, someone has dropped out at short notice. Hurry up Martin, you mustn't miss the first lesson." Martin was rushed to the SUV, handed Flora's vaccination papers, lead and poo bags. Flora was placed in the travelling cage at the back. A white-faced Martin drove out of the courtyard.

"Why do I feel that we are waving him off to his first day at school? I feel so nervous for him," I said. When Tenby arrived at the Priory, Flora and my cat Cleo became friends. I agreed to have her, but on the condition that I would get help with walks, and puppy training. Martin had promised to undertake puppy classes.

"Or an execution," said Jim. "It's a good

thing he's rushed off like that, saves him getting even more worried beforehand. Don't worry Daisy, it'll do them both good. You had to make a stand and have help to cope with her." I nodded. But my stupid guilt and eager to please mentality, still had me worried over Martin.

We trooped into the kitchen. I opened my bag, giving Jim his evidence, then put the kettle on for my mug of tea. I always drank tea, I love the smell of coffee but coffee didn't love me. The others automatically filled their mugs from the coffee pot, which was always on the go. After we had all greeted the dog and her pups of course! They looked happier, more alert. The mother was watching us now with renewed interest. Jim smoothed the paper out and copied the names down in his notebook.

Maggie came over and looked over his shoulder. "We found it on that path, beside that old bit of blanket. It's got names on it with dates beside them," explained Jim.

"Look! Some of them match the supplier's names I've got here," Sheila pointed to a list of names beside her. "These are for food and bedding. All these people deliver to this area. I pretended we needed deliveries at the Priory, as we are close enough to Hilltop farm."

"That was a great idea. Well done Sheila, you're right, some are definitely the same names," said Jim, comparing both lists.

"We may well need them anyway, the number of dogs we have now," I said sharply.

Jim gave me a look of sympathetic agreement.

"Yes, the delivery dates of two of them coincide. The other names don't mean anything though. Well, that only leaves the pub for immediate investigation. Especially as it's Saturday tomorrow. Otherwise..." Jim was interrupted.

The screech of brakes in the courtyard, was followed by the slamming of a door. Maggie who had been standing by the window, gave a shriek of surprise which brought us all to our feet and rushing to her side.

"It's Martin! His lesson is an hour long. He's only been gone three quarters of an hour. What happened to him?" Maggie said.

"He never drives like that," I said, and I joined the others in a mad dash into the courtyard and out to Martin.

Martin was just getting Flora out of the cage and speaking soothingly to her.

"What's wrong?" Maggie said. She rushed up beside him and began helping him with Flora.

"Whatever's happened?" Sheila exclaimed.

Martin turned and faced us. He was holding Flora tightly in his arms who was licking his face, then she looked round at us and wagged her tail. Martin was no longer white faced, his face was scarlet.

"We were expelled! Yes, on our first lesson! After fifteen minutes! Flora and I were expelled from the puppy class!" shouted a furious Martin. He never raised his voice and was always calm. Not now! No one had ever seen

Martin in such a rage. Even his wispy beard seem to stiffen and bristle with fury.

"What did she do?" asked Sheila.

We waited in silence, but I saw lips twitching,

"A nasty little dachshund puppy kept nipping Flora's tail and back leg. The teacher didn't see that. She saw Flora when she turned and growled at the puppy after the fifth nip! She warned us! And she sent us to the naughty corner!" Martin patted Flora, and she licked him again. Taking a deep breath, he blurted out. "Another dog was called Flora, and it's owner and nasty son kept dancing round it, calling the name Flora again and again!"

"Oh no," I said. My hand flew up to my mouth. I knew it was awful for poor Martin. But it did have its funny side.

"Oh yes! Our Flora kept rushing towards them and jumping up at them in excitement. So, the woman in charge, just told us to leave. We were expelled!" Martin stared at us. We couldn't help it, we just erupted into laughter. Each one, tried not to laugh, but it was impossible.

"Quiet Martin and timid Flora, expelled from puppy class on the first lesson," giggled Sheila.

"And the class had just started," snorted Jim.

"Come on Flora, you deserve a drink and a biscuit." I reached out and took hold of the puppy.

"And you Martin, need a drink and a slice of cake," said Maggie. She linked her arm with his and propelled him into the kitchen.

After a large whisky, unusual for Martin, especially at that time of day and a large slice of chocolate cake, Martin sat back in his chair.

"I suppose it is funny. It wasn't at the time," he said slowly. His hand ran through his long brown hair, which was now completely dishevelled. His face was still flushed after the mornings events. He looked round at us. We were all trying to look sympathetic but struggling not to laugh. Martin smiled, and then he too was laughing.

"I can imagine. It was horrible for you, as well as Flora," I sympathised.

"We do understand and sympathise with you Martin, but you must agree, it does have its funny side," Sheila patted his arm.

Flora had investigated the new arrivals. Snuffles and sniffs over with, she climbed into the box and was fast asleep beside them. Her first trip to puppy class had been exhausting!

"Oh, I almost forgot. At the beginning of the class, everyone arrived and chatted to each other. I heard some," here Martin grinned at Sheila, "interesting 'Intel' about the puppy farm!"

CHAPTER FIVE

"Now you tell us!" Sheila cried. "Come on then, what intel did you hear?" She bounced up and down in her chair, her tight white curls dancing each time. Eyes alight with excitement, she grabbed Martins arm and shook it. "Tell us!"

"There was a lady who had another dachshund. That was a lovely puppy, Lottie, who liked Flora. She said that she got the pup from an advert in the local paper. She met a nice little old woman in a layby on the A 30. The puppy was supposed to be one of a litter, that her daughter had bred. The old woman said her daughter was moving house and couldn't join them as promised with the pup's mum."

"Didn't she think that was all a bit suspicious?" Jim asked. He frowned at this story and shook his head at such folly.

"It was meant to be a halfway meeting place for both of them. She'd been promised that the mother would be with the pup, but she was only shown photos. The old woman said that she'd forgotten the pup's papers and promised to send them to her when she got home."

"They never came," I said, knowing that also had been a lie.

Martin shook his head. "No, the vet said it hasn't had a healthy start, but will be okay with proper care. The owner is not very happy. She is furious about not having the papers.

The puppy was supposed to be a pedigree dog with an excellent background."

"That class was worthwhile, that was interesting information, or intel." said Sheila. She made us smile when she corrected herself with her new word.

"Alice must have been the sweet little old woman. She must have been involved with this business after all. Not as innocent as I thought," said Maggie. The disappointment at how Alice had deceived everyone was evident in her voice.

Martin's mobile rang. "Hello?" His eyes widened, and he pressed the loudspeaker button, and placed it on the table, motioning us all to listen. "Hello, yes it's Martin speaking." We all leant forward to listen.

"Hello Martin. It's Gail here, from the puppy class this morning. I've just finished the class. I've spoken to some of the mums and dads of the sweet little puppies."

"Hello Gail," Martin's voice was cautious. His face had darkened, and he was shrinking within himself as if expecting a blow.

"Mums and dads?" Jim muttered, his eyebrow raised. Sheila shushed him and dug an elbow into his side. He grunted but kept quiet.

"I've got to apologise to you and to darling Flora. I didn't realise that your little poppet was called Flora. That woman and her son were completely out of order shouting their puppy's name all the time, especially as it was your pup's name as well. Another mum told me that Siegfried the dachshund was also naughty and kept nipping Flora." At this point, we were all struggling to keep quiet. We were shaking with mirth at this phone call, and at Martin's face. "So, Martin, can you and Flora, the little poppet, forgive me. Will you come back next week? Do say you'll come back."

All our heads nodded in unison, and after a pause, Martin agreed. He closed his phone and glared at us.

"Why are you all laughing? Why did you make me agree?"

"It was Gail's choice of words, you being Flora, the little poppet's daddy! She was..." Words failed Sheila and she doubled up in giggles.

"Never mind, that's good news Martin. You got great information for us, you're bound to pick up more," Jim said.

"That's if I go back. I'm not sure I want to. All those pups and people, and me trying to keep an eye on Flora," mumbled Martin. There was a silence around the table. Martin was a real introvert. It had been difficult enough for him to attend the class. To be singled out and expelled in front of everyone must have been his worst nightmare. I could understand his reluctance at returning. It had taken some time for him to let down his defences with us and feel at ease in the group.

"How about me going with you?" Maggie said. Martin's face lit up with delight.

"Would you? That would be great. I could manage it then," was the eager reply.

"I think that will double our chances of getting gossip if Maggie goes with Martin. Great idea," said Jim with enthusiasm. "Let's go to the pub this evening, I think that may be our next avenue to explore." He looked around at us for approval.

"Davies goes on a Saturday," said Maggie. "Should we go if he's not there?"

"Yes, it may look suspicious if we only go that one night. If we go tonight, it will be familiar to us. We may be able to chat to people, without him realising that we are checking up on him." Jim said.

"Who's going to drive?" Sheila asked.

"I'll drive," I said. As the only teetotal person, I was always a designated driver. I'm certain that's why my husband stayed married to me for so long.

The pub sat back from the road. It was in a valley at the bottom end of the village. Dark woods loomed above and behind it, and a fast-moving stream raced down the valley before it. A scruffy unkempt car park with faded signs and chipped paintwork were not promising. Surprisingly, although shabby, the inside of the pub was clean, glasses and optics sparkling. A large fire in an inglenook fireplace gave out a welcome warmth. Maggie, Jim, and Martin chatted ales and beers with a large man behind the bar. Sheila and I wedged ourselves into the back of a large table. Faded, well-worn carpets, matched the outdated bench seating and chairs. A couple of men stood at the far end of the bar. They eyed us suspiciously, then pointedly ignored us.

"Doubt we'll get any gossip from them," muttered Sheila to me.

I laughed, "definitely not the chatty type."

The others came over, glasses in hand. Still talking about the qualities of the ales and beer, they sat down at the table. Sheila had a gin and tonic. I got my mineral water bottle, and an empty glass. Neither of us had been offered ice or lemon. There was talk between us, general subjects in case anyone listened to us. Jim had us well-trained I thought.

"One last drink?" Jim said. The disappointment on his face was obvious. We had achieved nothing by this visit. There were nods of agreement and he and Martin rose to their feet. Jim and Martin walked back with the refills, for the others, not for me. One mineral bottle of water on a winters evening is enough!

An elderly couple walked in. They were both small, and shabbily dressed, obviously pensioners, and obviously local by the friendly greetings they got.

"The police have gone at last," said the woman to the landlord. "Thank goodness! Men tramping about next door, and all over the front and back garden. The noise they made inside the house next door was dreadful. Don't want to be bothered by that nonsense anymore." A well-worn winter coat was tied around her dumpy figure. A battered hat had been thrust onto her head as protection against the squally rain. Her husband wore faded dungarees, an ancient wax jacket, and a scarf tied tight around his scrawny neck. Wispy hair had been ruffled by the wind, and his constant movements by his hand, did little to smooth it down.

"But Alice didn't die there, did she? Thought she had a fall on that path she always took home," said the landlord.

"Yes. Why they had to come next door to us, for all that length of time, beats me. We heard that fat policeman talking," said the woman.

Glances were exchanged between us. The fat policeman had to be Tenby.

"You hiding behind the hedge again," laughed one of the two men at the bar.

"I was out seeing to my garden. No crime in that, is there? Couldn't help but overhear him. Loud booming voice he has!"

"Well, go on, don't mind those two, what did you hear?" Urged the barman.

The whole pub went silent. She looked around, relishing her moment, the focus of all eyes.

"He said it were no accident. He'd just had a phone call, she'd been drugged and thrown off that path, down the hillside. They were going to go up again to where it happened, to look for more evidence."

She sank down onto a barstool, and glanced round again, a triumphant grin on her face. I felt like applauding. Her news had silenced every single person in that bar.

"Drugged? That's premeditated murder. This is getting serious," Jim whispered.

The general conversation drifted away from the murder. Lack of rain was a problem, unusual despite the cold weather this winter. Then football became the ongoing topic. This was obviously going to last all night. Even the old woman had something to say about her favourite team.

"The police are no longer at the cottage. It's not a crime scene anymore. Who's game for investigating?" Jim said in a low voice. That previously disappointed look had fled from his face.

"Go and break into a dead woman's cottage?" Martin shuddered at the very idea.

"Why not? The police have done their search and found any forensics they need. It's not as if we're going before them. And it's not a crime scene!" Jim argued.

Maggie drained her glass and thumped it on the table. "But it's still breaking and entering…" her voice faded away. An anxious look spread over her normally cheerful countenance.

"What exactly do you hope to find? What are you looking for?" I asked, earning an approving nod from Jim. I don't know why. I wasn't keen on this idea at all. The reasons for this illegal project should be important, not some hare brained venture on Jim's part.

"Anything we can find connecting her to the puppy farm. It's a specific link we are after.

Tenby isn't going to go down that road of investigation. He's looking for a murderer. We're looking for a puppy farm, it's totally different." Jim stated. But he didn't look at me. He stared into his glass. No way was that the whole scenario in Jim's mind. Jim had another agenda in his mind, I was sure of it. He wanted to find the puppy farm, but I felt certain he fancied himself catching the actual murderer.

I put down my half-drunk glass of mineral water. I was gasping for a cup of hot tea. Jim would go, with or without us. He was good at spy type stuff. He'd never admit it, and would hate me for even thinking it, but he was slowing down. He needed help, no, that was the wrong word. He needed backup.

"When do we go?" I asked him. I was now resigned to the fact I was about to embark on a career of breaking and entering!

"Now!" Jim said and rose to his feet.

CHAPTER SIX

The lane was dark. Night had closed in, and the heavy cloud cover, and intermittent beams of moonlight gave an ominous feel to our actions. Martin especially had gone quiet, the hand stroking his beard was trembling. Only Sheila was enjoying herself. Her eyes glittered with excitement, and her eagerness was apparent in her leaning forward in anticipation.

We arrived at the cottage. Far too soon for my liking. Jim parked the SUV further along from the cottage.

"You wait in the SUV Martin with Sheila. Take the wheel and be ready to move quickly," said Jim. Maggie and I got out and walked along the lane with Jim. "Not the front door. We'll go round the back, down the side path," whispered Jim. He led the way, the slim light from his phone showing the neat path with its edging of dormant lavender plants. After Jim did his work with his trusty lock picking tools, he slowly eased the back door open. "Okay, keep your torches pointed downwards. We may be in the depths of the countryside, but there's always the chance of some insomniac about." We followed him in. It was a surreal feeling, standing in an empty cottage, knowing that the woman who had left only that morning was never coming back. Add the fact that we were committing an illegal action and my emotions were in overdrive! "Can you two search upstairs? I'll start down here."

Maggie and I crept up the stairs. A worn stair carpet led into dingy and depressing bedrooms. One small room had an unmade single bed. On it, was a pile of folded bedding. The other bedroom had just an empty bed, no bedding, nothing.

"I'll check in the cupboards and drawers in this room," Maggie said.

"Okay, I'll do the other room." It was surprisingly free of clutter. Somehow, on hearing about Alice, I'd imagined ornaments, photographs, and dainty mats everywhere. No, there was one armchair, two bedside cabinets and a large, huge oak wardrobe. The dressing table was bare. "This is so odd," I muttered to myself. I stood still in the middle of the room, playing the beam of my torch around. "There's nothing, no pictures, and nothing on any surface. It's so strange," I repeated.

"What's strange?" Jim's whisper came from the doorway.

"This room. It's empty, there are no personal objects. It's like a hotel room, where the guest has just checked out."

Jim walked in and stood beside me. His torch swept round the room. "Yes, you're right."

"I've not opened any drawers or the wardrobe." I walked towards one of the bedside tables and opened a drawer. "Nothing," I said.

"The wardrobe is empty as well," said Jim,

opening its door.

Maggie joined us. "There are boxes downstairs, in the front hall. They hold personal mementos, photographs, ornaments and clothes. Everything is packed up. She was ready to move out," she said.

"How could we find out where she was planning to move to?" Maggie asked.

"Jasper!" Jim and I said in unison. We had used the young estate agent to get information in our last escapade. He had shown us round cottages, especially the one we were keen to see. We had suspected a dead body had been hidden there. It had!

"My niece again?" I asked.

"Why not? She is very fussy, and she is still looking for the right cottage!" Jim smiled at me.

"Poor Jasper, I don't think he'll be happy to see us again," I said.

"There's nothing personal downstairs. Only in the boxes. She'd obviously cleared it all, ready to move out and..."

My phone rang. All three phones rang. "Car coming down the valley! Get out now!" Sheila's text messages galvanised us into action. It only took a few seconds to race down the path, whilst Jim locked the back door behind us.

The SUV doors were open for us. We dived in and slammed the doors.

Martin drove fast, feeling his way up the hill, not even putting on his headlights. At the top of the hill, Martin stopped the car and began shaking. "Can someone else drive?"

"Move over Martin, I'll drive," I said. Getting out from the back seat I walked round the car.

"Thanks Martin, that was quick thinking of yours. Fast getaway, with no lights, well done," Jim said. Martin always nervous, looked pleased at Jim's praise. His shaking stopped, and he gave us a weak smile.

I took my place in the driving seat and settled myself back in it. We all looked down the valley towards the cottage. In a sudden shaft of moonlight, we could see the car come to a halt in front of the cottage. A figure got out, pushed open the gate and proceeded to the front door.

"Do you think that's Tenby?" I asked.

"Could be, that's one bulky guy going in," said Sheila. "That Tenby guy is overweight."

"He'd be fine, if he got the right food to eat, and then he'd lose weight." Maggie said defensively. I thought to myself, she likes him.

"Did you find anything? What did you discover?" Sheila asked impatiently, as we sat watching the man walk up the path.

"She had cleared everything out. There were only some boxes in the hall containing photographs and mementos. They were all packed for the removal men. Alice had been ready to go." Maggie had turned towards Martin and Sheila as she spoke.

"Shall I go straight home?" I said, preparing to drive off.

"Poor Daisy, no wonder you're keen to get home. A cold drink of water on a miserable night is not very pleasant. Don't worry Daisy, we'll have a chocolate chip cookie, and a large mug of tea for you when we get home." Maggie said.

"After a little breaking and entering on the way home I think I need a couple of chocolate chip cookies!" I grumbled.

Martin had stopped on the brow of the hill. The road circled around at that point before going downwards towards the valley and the Priory. The whole valley lay before us and the two cottages were almost directly beneath us. The old couple had obviously left their porch light on, and it cast a feeble glow at the front of the semi-detached cottages.

"That was successful in one way." I said. "We broke in and got out with nothing going wrong, and no excitement." I relaxed into the driving seat, relieved at the outcome of the night's adventure. Putting my hands on the steering wheel, I prepared to drive back to the Priory.

I spoke far too soon!

CHAPTER SEVEN

The earth shook, and the SUV rocked. The cottages in the valley below exploded into a huge fireball. We clung on to anything we could reach as the SUV rocked, and the earth around us shook.

"What the..." Jim exclaimed.

"Oh my God!" Sheila shrieked.

"Tenby! Do think that really was...?" Maggie squeaked.

The outbursts from everyone at once, shattered the stunned silence that had initially engulfed our car.

"Shall we go and help?" Sheila whispered.

"No!" The harsh flat voice was Jim's. "Daisy drive! Get us back to the Priory as fast as you can. Oh Daisy! Why did you say we'd had no excitement? I'll swear that you wish stuff to happen to us!"

"I don't wish any excitement upon us! I don't!" My response was automatic. I gave a last look down the valley at the burning cottages and tightened my grip on the steering wheel, my knuckles whitening as I did so. With my teeth clenched, I drove off down that Cornish winding lane as fast as I dared.

"But shouldn't we have..." Sheila began, her voice quavering at the shock.

Jim patted her arm, "I know you want to help. The police and ambulance will be there in no time. It's the trained professionals that are needed. We would only be in the way. What could we do? How would we explain our presence there? The police will find out that we were in the pub tonight asking questions about Alice and Davies. If they found us at the cottage..." his voice tailed away.

"That could have been us, how did we escape the explosion?" I said. The full horror of what might have been, hitting me in earnest.

"What triggered the explosion? Why didn't it explode when we..." Maggie gave a sort of gulp but couldn't finish what she was saying. Why didn't Jim see it, she meant.

"I've been going over everything in my mind. Everything we touched, everywhere we went. I saw nothing suspicious," Jim said in a flat voice.

I glanced across at him. In the dim light I could see the shock etched upon his face and something else. I realised that it was fear, at how close he had brought us to our deaths. "What about the boxes in the hall? Maggie and I thought they were the last lot to go with her. We had a quick glance in the first box, but that was only her clothes."

"Someone knew she was going to make one last visit to the cottage. They were determined, to make it her last visit anywhere." Jim said. An uneasy silence grew in the SUV. There was a heavy horror engulfing all of us. Each of us, in our own way, was trying to come to terms with the terrible act we had just witnessed. Each of us, of the three that had entered the cottage, realised how near to death we had been. I said nothing. I knew my face was probably white and strained, the others were in the eerie light of the car considerably paler than they had been earlier. Determination had me crouched over the steering wheel. I was going to get us home. I was going to get us home as fast as I possibly could. I expected that once I arrived home, I'd probably collapse into a quivering wreck.

"The front door! It was attached to the front door! That's where the trigger mechanism and the bomb was rigged. We broke in through the back door, that saved our lives!" Jim said.

"Could that have been Tenby? We only saw a largish figure walking up the path. Could it have been someone else? Perhaps it wasn't him?" Sheila finally put into words the thoughts that were in all our minds. Her voice shook a little, and she gave a small sob.

"You're right Sheila, it was dark, and we only caught the briefest glimpse of a bulky figure. It could have been anybody at all, the light was in front of him, and maybe that made the figure look larger..." I couldn't finish speaking.

It was Martin who spoke into the silence. His voice rose in excitement, "that wasn't Tenby's car! It was the wrong shape altogether, I'm certain it wasn't his car."

"I hope you're right Martin," Maggie's voice came out in a breathy rush, "I only hope you're right."

The kitchen lights were all on. It was very

bright, and warm from the Aga. Trooping in from the SUV we had sat in our usual chairs. Somehow, we needed every light on. I had gone to the kettle to make my usual cuppa.

"Let me do it Daisy. I want to keep busy. Stop the worrying getting out of hand." Maggie said pushing me to one side.

That had been a couple of hours ago. I had checked on Cleo and Flora, whilst Maggie had made my tea. They were not only fine, but annoyed that I disturbed them. A few treats, and I was forgiven. When I returned to the kitchen, Maggie gave me my tea, and a plate with the two promised chocolate chip cookies. I noticed the others had not only cookies, but also fruitcake.

"There is fruitcake for you as well Daisy, and it's buttered." Maggie grinned at my delight, as she passed me my slice of fruitcake with fresh farmhouse butter.

"My Mum always buttered her fruitcake, and now I've got into the habit. I've never met anyone else who likes it this way," I said. I sat down, cradled the hot mug of tea in my hands and stared down at my two plates with pleasure. Then I thought of the explosion. Sheila's hand came out and grasped my shaking hand. With her help, my mug made it safely onto the kitchen table. Just! Only a small amount of tea slopped over onto the table. Suddenly, I shook all over. The death of that man, and there was little doubt that he could have survived that blast, swept over me again. But it was the realisation that it had been purely by chance, that it hadn't been us, overwhelmed me.

"Daisy, drink your tea and eat something." Jim ordered me in his military voice. Normally, I'd have argued at that tone, but now I did as he told me. I felt better. Was it the chocolate chip cookies or the buttered fruitcake? I felt reaction begin to take hold of all of us. Martin was constantly shaking his head, Jim was drumming his fingers, his face dark with anger.

Maggie looked at me. "Where are the pups and Maisie going to sleep?"

"I'm sorry, but not with me. Cleo decided she'd have Flora with us. I doubt she'd accept this lot," I said.

"I agree Daisy, but I wondered if they should stay in this kitchen or the old back Priory one?"

"In this kitchen. It's got the Aga on 24/7. They will be a lot warmer in here. What about fencing them off in that corner up there?" Jim said.

"That's a great idea, this kitchen is massive. Will you and Martin manage some sort of run for them?" Maggie asked.

"There's a news bulletin coming on the local radio. Quiet. Let's listen," said Martin.

There was the mention of a fire that had broken out in a cottage. That was all. No talk of explosion, or of casualties.

"Useless! No information at all. What we need are more details about the actual explosion itself," mumbled Jim.

"Shall we call it a night and go to bed?" Sheila asked. We all shook our heads.

"Would anyone like a nightcap?" Maggie suggested.

"A nightcap is a great idea," Jim said.

Not one of us wanted to leave the kitchen. No one wanted to go to bed. We all knew that we'd see etched on our minds, the image of the man. He stood under the glare of the old couple's porch light, for a while, before entering the cottage. He must have been breaking in, I thought. That's why he was outside the door for those few minutes. Then he had entered. As he did so, the flash had lit up the entire valley. Waves of sound echoed around the hills, ricocheting from the granite rocks to the valleys below. No one could have survived. Who had the man been? That's why we sat. That is why we ate and drank mechanically. Each one of us, was hoping and praying that it had not been Tenby.

"I can't go to bed until I know. Same for all of us, isn't it?" I said.

There were nods of heads, but no one else spoke. We sat on in silence.

Martin jumped to his feet. "A car! I hear a car."

He dashed to the window. He peered out across the courtyard to the archway. Headlights entered and flashed across the kitchen window. Everyone joined Martin and stared out of the window.

CHAPTER EIGHT

"Flora! She's barking!" My voice broke into the silence that had engulfed us all after Martin's words.

"Tenby must be there!" Sheila cried.

"He must have been in the car that's just driven into the courtyard." Maggie whispered, her hand to her mouth in relief.

Flora, or Fluffy as she was originally called had lived with Tenby for a few weeks. That initial time with Tenby had given Flora a deep love for him. She always greeted him enthusiastically, no matter how late the hour of his return. Barking even from her bed, she always knew his footsteps in the courtyard. It could be irritating for me, especially if he was late home!

"Why are we up so late?" I asked. I could see Tenby's bulky figure pausing in the courtyard to call a greeting to Flora. "What excuse have we got? Do we say that we saw the explosion?" The others stared at me in astonishment, then an increasing realisation dawned on them.

"Of course, how stupid of me. Daisy you are right! We can't let Tenby know that we saw him at the cottages..." Jim began.

"Or thought we saw him," I corrected Jim. "That couldn't have been Tenby we saw.

"Why are we up so late?" I asked again.

"We couldn't sleep after the noise and sight of the explosion. We saw it on our way home from the pub." Jim stated in a flat tone. He had recovered from that lapse of forethought but was furious at himself at how he'd been affected by Tenby's possible death. Not professional, but what profession was it?

"Why were we at the pub?" Maggie said.

It was Martin who supplied the answer. "Because I swore I'd never return to the Red Lion. After that dreadful meal we had there, and especially the last time after the unfortunate incident with the murderer!"

"Yes, we are going to try several pubs. When we find one we like, that's going to be our local," Sheila said, embroidering the story.

"And that was the first," Maggie said, and nodded her approval of Martin and Sheila's story.

"Saw the lights on, you lot still up?" Tenby said walking into the kitchen.

"Yes, none of us could sleep after the death of Alice and that horrible explosion," Maggie answered.

"We hoped that you would be able to tell us something," said Jim.

"How do you lot know about the explosion?" A suspicious Tenby glowered at us beneath his shaggy eyebrows. He nodded at Maggie as she held up a glass and the whisky bottle.

"We were on a pub crawl!" Sheila declared with a gleeful smile at his horrified expression. "But we're taking it slow, only one pub at a time. Tonight, it was that pub down the valley," she added.

"Next time, we are going to try the other side of Bodmin," put in Martin "one a week, until we find one we can call our local. The Red Lion was our nearest, but never ever will I forget…"

"Okay, so how come you saw the explosion?" Tenby had no qualms about cutting into Martin's rant about the Red Lion. He, like us, had heard Martin go on at length about it, especially about the 'night of the cauliflower' as I privately christened it.

"We left the pub and took the route along the valley, and up onto the moor. We were just on the brow of the hill when the cottages went up," said Jim.

"We would have gone back down to help, but Jim said we'd only get in the way," said Maggie.

"Jim's right. Nothing anyone could have done. The old couple were in the pub, so they were okay," Tenby said. No one spoke. There was a silence as we all waited. Who was it that triggered the explosion? What had happened to him? We waited. After the pause, Tenby continued. "There was a fatality though. Some sort of handyman who had called at other cottages in the village during the day. No one knew him, or anything about him. It's an ongoing investigation, as to what caused the explosion." The whisky glass was drained and placed on the table. "Thanks Maggie. I've got an early start tomorrow, I've got a car calling for me, mine broke down at lunchtime and is sitting in the garage awaiting repair. I'm away to my bed. Good night all." He left the kitchen, and his heavy footsteps could be heard crossing the courtyard. The key in his door turned, and the door firmly shut behind him.

Then the whole lot of us began speaking.

"Well?" Jim said.

"He knows," I said.

"Yes, I think he suspects that we'd been in the cottage. And I think he's pleased about it. Not only that, but he's also been pretty free with tonight's information. Not like him at all. He wants us to investigate, because I think he's stumped by this case," said Jim.

"He wants our help without asking us for it!" Sheila said.

"Why? Why this case? Why is this case so important that he wants help from all of us?" I asked.

"Flora!" Maggie and Sheila said in unison.

"He can't bear the thought of those poor puppies and their mums being ill-treated. He loves dogs and can't bear the thought of any cruelty towards them." Sheila said.

"Nor can I," said a grim-faced Jim. "That puppy farm must be closed down!"

"The Priory Five are going to put a stop to this evil bastard and his cruel trade!" Sheila declared.

Solemn faced we agreed and rose to go to bed. Tomorrow this investigation would begin in earnest.

CHAPTER NINE

The morning air was cold, and my breath came out clouds as I walked with Flora. We had left Cleo attending to her business with great distaste in the cold frosty garden.

When we got ready for the walk, Cleo had sat on the window seat, watching Flora's antics with horror. I wasn't too happy either.

"Flora, please sit still whilst I get your harness on. I know you love your walks, and you're very excited." She rolled over on her back, tail wagging furiously. Flora was an elusive fluffy ball. The puppy training class, her second one, was later today. Maggie was going with Martin, I knew he wouldn't have gone back otherwise. Flora's expulsion from the puppy class last week had really upset him. I didn't blame him, it would have been embarrassing for anyone, let alone an introvert like Martin.

My footsteps crunched on the frost. I breathed in the sparkling air with wonder. Each morning, the sweeping vistas of moorland and patchwork of stonewalled fields confirmed my decision to stay here. My walk in the beautiful surroundings and Flora's antics occupied my immediate thoughts. At the back of my mind, however, was the worry of the murder of Alice, and the explosion last night. We had found boxes and suitcases in the hallway of her cottage. The pups and their mum had been hidden from view high on the hill. Obviously, Alice was leaving. She was running away and taking the dogs with her. Why? Why now? What had prompted this sudden flight? Did it have anything to do with Davies? Or was it completely unconnected with him and the puppy farm? No! It had to be connected with the puppy farm. Otherwise, she wouldn't have hidden the dogs. This was hopeless. I stopped my rambling train of thought. Conjecture was useless without facts. We needed facts and more information. Every avenue seemed to have been closed off to us. Our usual methods were no use now. Sheila couldn't meet Alice at her knitting group. There was no cottage left for us to visit with Jasper.

"Come on Flora. Let's go home. Perhaps the others will have ideas for us to investigate."

Flora tired from the excitement of her walk, was soon asleep in her basket. Cleo stalked over to the basket and sniffed the tired puppy. She joined her in the basket, washing the puppy, before she too settled down for a sleep. I took off my boots, jacket, gloves, hat, and I threw on a heavy knit cardigan. Another of my bold buys. Orange and pink stripes clashed in a huge chunky knit. Warmest of all my cardigans, its vivid colours always cheered me up on a wintry day. I grabbed my phone and keys.

"Won't be long, just off to the Priory kitchen for a coffee," I told my pets. When I locked my door, I thought perhaps I was being stupid. Fancy telling the animals where I was going, and how long I was going to be!

Jim sat in his usual spot. His back was to the wall, with all the windows and doors facing him. Once a spy, always a spy, I thought to myself. Jim always insisted he was a civil servant. No civil servant that I knew carried a gun, had another gun holster on his ankle, lock picking tools in his wallet, and a burner phone. My friend Elsie had wanted me to join her in her bungalow community in Bournemouth. She had mentioned bingo, musical singalongs, 60s nights, and afternoon tea dances. The friends she mentioned, sounded a collection of dreary people, old before their time. I'll bet no one there carried a gun!

Sheila limped into the kitchen with a grin on her face. An avid computer gamer, she took on and beat many young ones. Despite her eighty-six years, she embraced every nuance of technology. No sitting down with a bingo card for Sheila!

"I found some information last night." She plonked herself down on the chair. "There is a dog food company delivers weekly to this area. I emailed them, a false email stating I was a dog boarding kennels. They will deliver to me the same time that they deliver to Hilltop farm. I've got a list of their dog foods, but it will have to be a sizeable order."

Jim looked at the dog in the basket with her

two pups. Then he looked at Maggie and Jim who were getting ready to take Flora to puppy class.

"I rather think we will be needing sizeable orders. Give the list to Maggie, please Sheila. Maggie can ask the trainer which food she recommends, and about the delivery company. Great work Sheila. I thought we had no leads at all, but you managed to find one."

Sheila's grin nearly split her face in two. I loved her enthusiasm.

"Great sleuthing, Sheila. It gives me a great excuse to chat with the dog trainer." Maggie said as she pocketed the list and made for the door.

"Before you both go. What about tonight? It's Saturday, so Davies may well be there as usual. Shall we go to the pub tonight?" Jim asked the two standing at the doorway, and then looked at me and Sheila. We all agreed, and it was settled. Tonight, we would return to the pub. I only hoped that there would be no explosions on the way home. After the departure of Martin and Maggie, we had gone our separate ways.

Saturday in Stonebridge was always busy, winter and summer. Shopping and any other outings were best done during the week. Without realising it, I had drifted into a routine in my cottage. Weekends were becoming my housework and catch up days. My washing was in the machine, the kitchen floor washed, and the lounge vacuumed and dusted.

"It was great!" Martin smile was broad when he popped in with Flora at my back door. "Everything went well, and we have lots of info. Jim said to save it for our chat in the pub tonight. Davies goes early, about six, and leaves about eight. After he leaves the pub, we will go for fish and chips." Martin left, his cheerful smile and brisk walk was in marked contrast to his previous demeanour. On our initial meetings, Martin had been an introvert. He'd seemed to hunch over and speak haltingly, whenever he did speak. The Priory and Flora had been good for him, so far!

"See you at the pub crawl tonight!" I had smiled at Martin. My smile faded when he was out of sight. This visit tonight to the pub, was not something that I was looking forward to. The previous night's experience had been difficult for me to cope with. I was dreading this evening. Somehow I knew that it would not pass off peaceably. I just knew that there would be trouble. I could only hope that no one would die!

CHAPTER TEN

Flora was in the lounge asleep on the sofa. Flat on her back, her exhaustion after the puppy class, was obvious. She had each paw in the air. Cleo jumped up beside her. She sniffed all the other puppy smells from Flora's fur, and gave a meow of distaste, and jumped down. Walking over towards the window seat she jumped up, washed herself from tip of her tail to her nose, in case of puppy contamination, and glared at me.

"It's not my fault she smells of other puppies," I said. Realising how stupid that was, I reached for my book. "Ridiculous, reading into a cat's movements its feelings and accusations," I muttered. "And now, I'm talking to myself!" I opened my book, but my thoughts drifted away. The lines of words danced across the page. They blurred, as yet again my thoughts wandered back to the cruel murder of Alice. She had seemed to be an inoffensive little woman. Or had she been a cruel puppy farmer? Had she an overwhelming appetite for money? Throwing my book down in despair, I went up to my study.

I had brought up a mug of tea with me. A very brightly coloured mug, in order to stop me dipping my paintbrush into it by mistake. I sat in front of my easel. After a few hours that had passed by — as if only minutes, I stretched. I looked at my watch in amazement. I rose and went to the window, the dramatic quality in the late afternoon sun over the moorland hills never failed to lift my spirits. The anxious shuffling sound behind me, alerted me to the fact that it was pet teatime.

"Okay, let me sort out my painting stuff, and I'll feed you both," I said. I rinsed out my brushes, carefully teasing each brush to a point. I wiped my palette clean of the muddy colours, whilst carefully preserving those unexpected mixtures of colours that sparked joy and were perfect for the next day's painting.

Sunflowers sat large on the pristine white hot pressed paper. I loved using a traditional Italian paper, one that had been used by the great artists since the thirteenth century. One sunflower was pale and unfinished. The other was throbbing with vibrant yellow, and an orange centre. My botanical paintings were never wishy-washy or faded looking. I loved the showy gaudy flowers in the garden. Beetroot, aubergines, and the creamy curls of cauliflower against brilliant green leaves were also perennial favourites of mine. The Art shop owner in Stonebridge had paintings for sale. After a conversation, he asked to see if mine would be suitable for sale. If this sunflower painting continued as well as I hoped it was going, I'd consider taking it in.

Two noses began poking my arm, followed by dabbing paws.

"Okay girls, let's go down and feed you."

They raced each other down the stairs. I always fed them in separate rooms. Otherwise, chaos ensued, each wanting some from the others dish. When they were finished, I opened the door between them. Each raced to the others dish, licking them clean. After they had a trip round the garden, I came in to get ready for our pub crawl. Well, one pub visit really, though pub crawl sounded better!

The pub looked dingier than ever in the twilight when we parked. On entering, the warmth and glow from the log fire was welcome.

"Back again? That's two nights running you've been in. Can't keep away, can you?" joked the landlord. His cheerful manner, the spotlessly clean bar and optics, and excellent beer on tap, explained the popularity of the pub. We sat again at the large round table under a window. I looked around. An elderly couple sat at a table beside the fire. I recognised them. They were the couple who lived next door to Alice. They looked tired and careworn and were obviously suffering from delayed shock. No wonder, I thought, their next-door neighbour murdered and their house blown up next day. That would shock anyone, let alone a couple of their advanced years. I kept thinking of them as the elderly couple, and advanced in years. It was a horrible shock to realise that they would only be a few years older than myself!

"When is your house going to get rebuilt?"

The landlord asked them.

"It'll take perhaps a year or more! We fixed up a static caravan at our daughter's place. It's cosy enough, even got central heating for the cold weather," answered the old woman.

"Terrible business," said the landlord, shaking his head. "Gas explosion, or something like that?" He was perpetually wiping down the bar and polishing glasses in between serving drinks and chatting to customers.

"We don't know yet. They took stuff to examine, evidence they call it," said the old man downing his half pint of beer. He reached for his wife's empty glass and made to rise.

"No, let me get these. They're on the house," said the landlord.

At the other end of the bar, sat a man nursing a pint of beer. Straggly dark hair was scraped across his scalp. Ferret like features with colourless eyes roamed around the room. They settled upon us. One swift glance was all he took. It was enough. Those emotionless eyes had glanced speedily over us but had taken in everything. It was only a glance, but I felt soiled by it, and fearful. Even from across the bar, the man gave off the smell of evil. He took a phone from his pocket and spoke softly. With the phone still in his hand, he wandered towards the window. He looked out and spoke again softly into the phone. The phone was closed and placed in his pocket. As he walked back towards the bar, he gave us a nod, and a strange smile.

"Looks like it's going to snow. Take care driving home." A dry chuckle came from his thin bloodless lips, and he returned to his seat at the bar.

The elderly couple rose, said good night to the landlord, and left. Ferret Face, sat still at the bar, nursing the one drink.

"He's listening and watching us," whispered Jim into my ear.

"Shall we get another drink?" asked Martin. Jim raised his glass to his lips, drained it, and replaced it on the table. He shook his head at Martin.

"Let's go, I'll drive tonight," he said, and looked round at each of us. "Okay with you Martin?"

There were murmurs of assent, and all glasses were emptied, except mine. My mineral water, as usual, was left half full.

"Fish and chips again? Or pizzas this time?" asked Martin as we got up from the table.

"Good night," said the landlord, still standing at the bar, still polishing glasses.

"Good night. Safe journey!" Ferret Face said as we passed him on his stool at the bar. His strange smile played about his lips, and as I walked past him, he gave another dry chuckle.

That man — I did not like. His attitude towards us was odd, and suspicious. But why did I feel like that? Why did I have that instinct that he meant us harm? There was no way he could hurt us, was there?

Maggie wanted pizza, Jim didn't care, Martin

wanted fish and chips, Sheila didn't mind. "You decide Daisy!" Maggie said.

I climbed into the SUV. As I fastened my seatbelt, I thought for a moment. "I'll go with Maggie, she does all the cooking for us. She can choose for tonight. It's pizza."

"Thanks Daisy, you and I can share the large veggie one," she grinned at me.

"Have you got enough fixings in?" Martin queried.

"Yes Martin, there's anchovies, capers, olives and tuna. Will that do?" Maggie replied. She rolled her eyes at me, and we both smiled at Martin.

"That's great. I love pizza with all the fixings," Martin said. He needed his 'fixings' for a pizza. The takeaway never had enough, or they were not the right ones. He was always most upset if Maggie had run out.

As Jim drove slowly out of the car park, I looked back and saw the figure at the window watching us. "Ferret Face has come to the window. He's watching us leave," I said.

"Ferret Face is a perfect name for him. He was staring at us all the time," said Sheila, craning her neck round for a last look at him.

"And listening. I saw him move along the bar closer towards us. He was eavesdropping," said Martin.

"I thought it creepy when he wished us a safe journey, he gave such a sinister chuckle afterwards," said Maggie.

"I noticed that!" Both Jim and I said in

unison.

Jim slowed down for a moment. "Okay, everyone make sure your seat belts are fastened. Hold onto something, make sure you're sitting straight. This is all in case I need to brake suddenly."

"You're expecting trouble?" When I said it, it was more of a statement than a question.

"I don't know. Alice's death was murder. We've been asking about Alice. To be on the safe side, I'll go slowly and sedately up and over that hill. If nothing happens, we'll have had a slow journey home, but..." His remark hung in the air. Each one of us checked our seatbelt. We all found something to hold onto. And we all braced ourselves. For what, we didn't know. But, as Jim said, it was better to be on the safe side.

We passed the gloomy fire ravaged derelict cottages. We drove further on up the hill. Now we were high above them, and the road narrowed, and twisted round the bends. We had reached the top of the hill. Moonlight showed the ruined chimneys beneath us, standing proud of the charred debris that had fallen about them. Jim slowed, as we all took a last look down.

It came out of nowhere. We realised afterwards that the tiny track leading up to the moor, had been his hiding place. A pickup truck, with large wheels and a grinning front metal grille came straight for us.

CHAPTER ELEVEN

Sheila gave a scream. Martin swore under his breath. I sensed rather than saw — everyone brace for impact. Not Jim. I knew he'd been alert. He had warned us to brace ourselves and hang on tight throughout the journey. Only a few moments before he'd warned us, yet again.

"I'm still going to take it slow and easy. If anything happens... If... You must all be ready because I'll take evasive action. Get ready to hold on tight. That guy has made me nervous." We took Jim at his word. On that journey up the hill, I noticed each and every one of us had white knuckles. It was the roar of the engine that had first alerted us. At a tremendous speed the truck charged down the lane, attempting to hit us broadside.

"He's going to push us over the cliff!" Maggie screamed.

"Oh no he's not! Hold on tight!" Jim shouted.

A screech of brakes, and the SUV swerved and shuddered sideways to a halt. The pickup truck only hit our bonnet a glancing blow. The driver in the pickup truck was unable to stop. His rapid speed down the incline meant that he could not halt the impetus of the truck over the cliff. We could see the brake lights come on, but he was already on the edge of the cliff. The shrieking and squealing of metal, accompanied by intermittent crashes, was swallowed in an explosive roar. The valley below us was lit up by a brilliant glare, which then died down to intermittent flashes. No one moved. Not one word was said. Frozen we sat, our breath coming from each of us in halting gasps and sighs. It was Jim who moved first, trying to extricate himself from the airbag. Martin, still enveloped in his airbag, was swearing creatively under his breath.

Maggie reached for her phone, "I'll call the police, and an ambulance." Her fingers trembling, struggled to press the correct keys.

I opened my door and got out. I had to hang onto the door, because my legs threatened to deposit me on the ground. They had turned to jelly, and I was shaking.

Jim joined me. "You okay Daisy? Sheila? Maggie?" He had jumped out of the car and rushed round checking on all of us.

I nodded. Sheila joined me, after slowly extricating herself from the back seat. "We are all fine, just shaken up," she said.

As one, we all moved to the edge of the cliff. We looked down the hillside in silence. Where we stood, the hillside plunged straight down to the valley floor. Metal debris was scattered in a pathway down to the flaming tangle of metal below.

"It was your skill and foresight Jim, that saved us. If it hadn't been for that, we'd have been down there, not him." Sheila patted his arm.

"Do you think...," whispered Martin, eyes wide as he joined us, staring down to the valley floor below.

"Not a chance. Don't feel sorry for him Martin. That's where he intended for us to go!" The harsh words from Jim hung in the air. The realisation of how true they were, caused us all just to stand in silence.

"Come on Sheila, it's cold, and we are all in shock. Let's get back in the SUV and wait for the police." I put my arm round the older woman's shoulders and guided her back to sit on the back seat. Sheila looked shaken, smaller, and somehow shrunken. Normally Sheila was cheerfully buoyant, but for once she'd been overwhelmed by events. Wordlessly she let me usher her into the back seat. Maggie joined us, leaving Martin and Jim to stare down the hillside to the valley floor. The wreckage still burnt. Sudden crackles were followed by the grinding of metal upon metal as it collapsed, accompanied by flickers of flame, and bursts of sparks high in the air.

"Where are the police? When will they arrive?" Martin kept repeating. He walked along the road, then walked back, restless in his attempt to lessen the shock. The eerie flickers from the valley floor died down. We were plunged into darkness. The night was silent but for the occasional owl call, and the scream of a fox. Then sirens could be heard approaching. There were cars, vans and suddenly men were rushing around. That flickering orange light in the valley, was replaced by the brilliance of police lights. The valley, and the hills above it echoed now with the shouts of men, and the noise of machinery.

"It would make my life easier if you lot would avoid this road! Two nights running and I've been called out here. And who should be sitting here? You lot!" Tenby was very much the policeman now. His voice was harsh. "What the hell has happened here?" At the sight of the damaged front bumper, and our deployed airbags, his face set into hard lines.

Jim stepped forward, of course it had to be Jim. I had to admit that he was good. Left to any of us, we would have stumbled and mumbled, repeated ourselves, and been unable to describe the sequence of events properly. Not so Jim, a succinct, coherent summary of events was narrated to Tenby. Jim took Tenby to the lane entrance. He showed him the muddy tyre tracks that had been coming straight down towards us.

"Okay, I see the evidence with my own eyes. I see it, what I want to know is why? Who was he? Why was your vehicle targeted?" Tenby asked Jim. Tenby walked over to the SUV and looked in at us. "You all okay? Any of you need to go to the hospital?" At our reassurances, he nodded. "What the hell have you lot been up to? It's obvious that you lot should be lying dead down there instead of that burning car. What are you investigating that is so bloody dangerous, that someone wants to kill you?"

All eyes turned to Jim. As our newly appointed chief negotiator with the police, and the one who suggested the pub outing, I felt it right he should reply.

"We went to the pub again," said Jim. No one else spoke. I could see even Jim was floundering to enlarge upon that remark.

I spoke. Well, someone had to! "We went to see if that chap Davies was in the pub. Nothing to do with the murder of Alice. We wondered if he was behind the puppy farm set up."

Tenby thought for a moment. "Did you speak to him?"

"No, last night we had asked questions about him. He wasn't there tonight. A chap with a Ferret Face was here tonight. He kept looking towards us, smiling to himself."

"That's right. He went to the window, looked out at the car park and then spoke on his phone," said Martin.

"Our SUV would have been the only unfamiliar car in the car park. Everyone else was local," said Jim.

"So, you think..." began Tenby.

"He phoned that guy and told him to push us off the road! He put out a hit on us. We were targeted!" Sheila cried out, her voice rising.

I looked at her sharply. Was she about to go into hysterics? Oh no! Not Sheila. She was not only excited. She was thrilled!

"Fancy that. Over eighty years old and having a mob hit put on me! That's great!"

CHAPTER TWELVE

Tenby told a policeman to take us home in a police car. "The SUV is needed in evidence and is in no fit state to take you anywhere. This will take some time to process here. Statements can be taken later tonight or tomorrow morning." It was a silent group that climbed in the police car. Slowly he drove past our battered vehicle and then along the valley edge. The burning vehicle was now a mass of glowing embers, with silhouetted figures moving about in the glare of police lights.

"No pizza or fish and chips then," said Martin.

"I couldn't eat anything. I don't know how you can think of food after what just happened Martin," said Maggie.

"We can go past the chippy, I've eaten nothing since this morning, I'm starving!" said the policeman.

"Won't you get into trouble?" Sheila asked.

"I won't tell Tenby, if you won't," was the reply.

Six fish suppers bought, and we entered the Priory courtyard. The police radio had burst into life as we did so.

"Stay with them. Don't let any of them out of your sight, Smithers."

"I have to check on my pets. Can I go to my cottage first?" I asked the policeman.

We all got out of the vehicle and stood around looking at Smithers, as he thought about it. "You lot go into the Priory, I'll stay with this lady while she checks her animals."

Cleo was asleep and did not want to be disturbed. Flora not only woke up but was delighted at the sight of a male visitor. Smithers crawling about on the floor enjoyed her greeting as much as she did!

"Come on Flora. You might as well come back to the Priory kitchen with me, or the policeman's and my fish and chips will get cold."

Flora and Maisie, and the pups played around the kitchen. We fussed over them, trying to take our minds off the horrific experience that we had gone through. I felt reaction begin to take hold. Martin was constantly shaking his head, Jim drumming his fingers, his face dark with anger. After a while the others went to the library.

The kitchen was empty, only Maggie was left. Tomorrow, I had planned my outing. Cleo could be left, I knew Maggie would pop in and feed her, take her out in the garden and make a fuss of her. As for Flora, she could come with me. "I thought I'd go out for the day tomorrow, do some sketches for my painting." Martin, Sheila, and Jim had gone into the library to check out Sheila's research. Smithers, the policeman had gone with them after he'd taken all our statements. They were all identical, and all very brief. We were glad to get them over with. Deliberately I'd waited until Jim had left the kitchen. Jim wouldn't have left my remark pass him by. Oh no, I knew him too well. He'd worry at my remark like a terrier with a bone.

"What a good idea Daisy. There are so many wonderful scenes for you to find for your paintings. Don't forget to wrap up warm. Shall I put up a picnic lunch for you?"

"Thanks Maggie, I'd love that. The area is so new to me, I thought I'd explore. I'll take some photos and make a few sketches. I can bring them home and work on them on wet and miserable days." I waffled on. Maggie smiled agreement. Jim and Martin always had breakfast at eight am, usually I arrived around eight thirty am. Tomorrow morning, I promised myself, I'd be breakfasted and gone from the Priory long before eight o'clock.

It was a brilliant sunny morning when I drove out of the Priory Courtyard at seven thirty. All my art stuff was in one big bag. The picnic lunch for myself and Flora was in another. Flora sat on a cushion at the back, strapped into her new doggy harness. Alert, she stared out of the side window. On previous trips she'd travelled in a cage. It was such a hassle, putting her in the cage, and then strapping it in securely. The other day I had realised that Flora was getting bigger and heavier. I'd also realised that I was getting older. An ideal solution was the dog harness, and she could jump in by herself!

That morning I photographed some beach scenes and drew a couple of rocky headlands. I'd stopped and parked on a layby on the moor to eat my lunch. I had given Flora a long walk first. The smells were exciting to her. It was with great difficulty I'd tried to stop her eating the tasty rabbit poo! When I returned Flora to the car, I walked over to an old, gnarled tree bent over with the prevailing winds. It had an incredible amount of lichen on it. All the sea and land scenes had been wonderful. But this lichen excited me with its delicate tracery and complexity. Only a green, grey colour, but the tones and depth of that colour were astonishing. I photographed it from every angle. I couldn't wait to get home and paint it.

Lunch was delicious, Maggie had packed chicken salad, crusty roll, and two of her flaky pastry mince pies. I was virtuous. I had everything except for that last mince pie. Whether it would survive the journey home... Then, and only then, when Flora was asleep on her cushion, the lunch rubbish packed for home disposal, did I open the bag on the passenger seat. Photocopies fluttered out of the folder. One was a copy of the photo from the frame Cleo had broken. The other was of a birth certificate that I had received in the post. I read them through for maybe the hundredth time, and then replaced them in the folder. My phone was working. The signal was good, so I googled the address found on the birth certificate. Somehow, I had been nervous about doing this. No putting it off now. After all

I was sitting here, with my free afternoon. The afternoon I had earmarked specifically to investigate the address. The map appeared, using my two fingers I enlarged it. I gazed out of the window. I didn't see the view. A deep breath, that's what I needed. One deep breath and I will look again to make sure. I knew that I didn't have to look again. But I did, just to be absolutely certain. I drove off, heading back towards the Priory, and the address.

The satellite map led me halfway down a country road, that was just marginally better than a track. I turned a bend and then I saw it. I parked some way uphill, looking down at the cottage. I compared the photocopy with the cottage before me. It was the same cottage, no doubt about it. The photo showed the wisteria in bloom. Now barefaced, it still grew up the walls. The branches, stick like traced the outline up around the windows towards the roof. The fence, no longer wooden palings, was now painted white, a boundary onto the lane. The bank beside which I parked, meant my van could not be seen. Flora had been restless while I was sitting. I had taken her out of the harness, and now she'd fallen into a deep sleep after the excitement of the day.

Compelled by some strange urge I got out of the van. Slowly I walked down the steep bank towards the cottage. My cautious approach, hoping to be unseen was a failure. The front door opened, and a woman came out and looked at me. She looked familiar, and I raised my hand to make an apologetic greeting, and say... what? No words came into my mind. It wouldn't matter if they had. There was no time to utter them.

"Go Sheba! Go Sheba!" shouted the woman. She glared at me. Turning, she went back into the cottage slamming the door behind her. I stood and watched as the large German Shepherd ran towards the gate. The gate was no barrier to her. She soared over it. Barking furiously, she bared her teeth, and ran straight towards me!

At first I couldn't move. I couldn't think. Realisation flooded in and I whirled round. The long grass tangled in my foot, and I slipped. It was wet and my ankle twisted violently, and I fell onto the ground. The pounding of heavy doggy footsteps grew ever nearer. The barks grew louder. I struggled to rise, my ankle causing me to cry out in pain. A tiny wet nose pushed into my face. Flora stood beside me. She turned and faced the oncoming dog and barked defiantly at it.

"Flora! Oh no Flora!" Fear for my puppy and myself, had me struggle into a sitting position facing the dog. I thrust Flora behind me, and kept a tight grip on her collar, as the huge dog grew closer.

CHAPTER THIRTEEN

The front door opened, only a crack. A piercing whistle echoed round the valley. The huge beast stopped immediately. I'll swear a look of intense disappointment swept over its massive face. One last sorrowful look at Flora and myself, with tail between her legs she loped back, and slipped through the front door. The door slammed shut behind her. I didn't move. Flora scrambled up to lick my face. I clutched her, half laughing, half crying.

"You silly little puppy! What a brave girl you are. You'd have been a mouthful for that monster!" I held her collar and tried to stand up. That was when I realised that I was in trouble. My ankle was swelling up as I looked at it. A tree nearby offered me a means of support. I crawled towards it, somehow managing to keep hold of Flora, and drag my bad ankle. I sat against it for a moment and took stock of my situation. This ankle would not take my weight on it at all. I looked back down at the cottage. Shuttered windows, tightly closed door in place, and dog within, meant no help would be forthcoming from there. "If I can reach the van Flora, we can get inside." My clothes were already muddy, and grass stained.

I dropped to the ground and crawled to my van door. Flora danced around me, yipping hysterically at this new game. The van door was ajar. That's how Flora got out I thought. Careless of me. It did mean I could haul myself up, and onto the seat. The pain in the ankle was so intense, I was scared that I might pass out. Flora jumped in and bounced across onto the passenger seat. I closed the van door behind me. Relief flooded over me. Safe within the van, and Flora secure beside me. I was so relieved and hugged her to me. She might have run off to enjoy this new freedom.

"You are such a good girl!" I sobbed into her fur. "No, this will not do!" I blew my nose hard and took a deep breath. "Flora, it won't do it all." I began to untie my trainer laces. I tried to slip my foot out of the trainer, but it was no good, the pain was so intense. My reach was also limited, not being as supple as I used to be. Nor as slim. Damn this getting old business!

I dialled Maggie's number. "Hi Daisy. I'm in Stonebridge shopping. I've just arrived at Tesco to do a big shop. Can I get you anything?"

"No, it's okay Maggie. See you later." I put the phone down. I thought and thought. I could not see any other way. My secret, my search, had been special just for me alone. I had hugged it to myself. If it had gone wrong, been a disaster, no one else would have known about it. Happy endings did not always happen. Life, family, and relationships could be messy. This I knew and was almost expecting. It would have been easier to bear if it had been my own secret disappointment. I sighed, I knew what I had to do. But that didn't mean to say I liked doing it. I dialled his number. It had to be Jim. Martin would only flap about and tell Jim anyway.

"Jim, I'm with Flora, down near the old bridge. I've hurt my ankle and I can't drive back."

"Martin and I will be there in ten minutes." That was Jim. I smiled to myself. No how? No why? Just, I'll be there in ten minutes.

It was nine minutes! Martin's car drove up and parked beside me. Both men jumped out and ran towards my van. Flora took one look at them and barked excitedly. This was turning out to be a fun day for her!

"Where's her lead?" Jim asked me. I put it on her, and he passed Flora out to Martin. "Walk Flora around Martin, whilst I see to Daisy." One look, from my tear stained face to my muddy knees and shoes, and he sighed. "Okay, turn around on the seat and put the bad ankle out towards me."

My trainer was eased off, and my swollen ankle inspected by Jim. "I don't know. There is a chance that it's broken, but it could be a bad sprain. What time is it?"

Lost in my intense scrutiny of my own ankle, it took a moment for his question to register. "It's nearly two thirty," I replied, puzzled at his question.

"Scoot over to the passenger side Daisy. Martin, can you take Flora back to the Priory? I'll run Daisy down to the village shop."

"I don't need any shopping..." I began to say. Had Jim lost the plot? Or had I?

"Why the village shop? Surely she needs the hospital?" Martin asked, obviously as puzzled as I was.

"The village shop has a surgery. If we hurry, I'll get Daisy in there in time before it finishes," Jim said.

"Oh right," Martin said, grinning at me. "You can pick up any shopping you need at the same time."

A modern shop built with funding and grants, it commanded a prominent position in the small village. The large car park and ramp leading to the entrance provided an easy hobble for me. There were a mixture of assistants in the shop. The post office was manned by paid staff who worked in one part of the building, whilst the shop itself was manned by volunteers. Jim had explained that there was a room designated for visiting doctors. I limped into the shop. Jim had to help me, much to my embarrassment. It was a relief to realise my socks were clean on that morning. Bright orange, they matched my red and orange sweatshirt. They also matched the tins of baked beans arranged in rows opposite to us. Good job I wasn't sitting in front of them, I would have been invisible. The array of tinned vegetables and tinned fish was quite comprehensive for a village shop. I noted that for future reference.

"What happened?" asked the elderly man beside me. The other occupants in the row, bent forward to get a better look at me and my ankle. "What did you do to your ankle?"

"I was walking my puppy near to the old bridge. The cottage door opened, and a huge German Shepherd ran towards us barking. I picked up the puppy, turned to run and twisted my ankle in the long wet grass."

"That's never Sheba! She wouldn't harm a fly," said the woman with the overflowing shopping bag.

"Sheba, yes that's the name. The woman whistled and called her name just as the dog reached us. But she set the dog on us deliberately." I began to shake again, the fright I had received still with me. I took a couple of deep breaths to calm myself, I couldn't let myself go in front of all these people, and in the village shop.

"Okay Daisy, calm down," the whispered words from Jim, and the surreptitious squeeze of his hand, did much to settle me.

"That looks nasty," said Jim. I looked at the man's thumb. It was swollen and underneath the nail it was black. "What did you do there?" Jim asked.

"Stupid mistake, bashed with a hammer. My own fault, but it hurts like the devil," replied the man.

The doctor came to the surgery door, behind a large woman who strode out muttering greetings to everyone in the row. The bad thumb man got up. He waved his bad thumb in front of the young doctor. The doctor looked at it, and then went to the counter. "A packet of needles and a box of matches please." He returned with his purchases, and ushered thumb man inside the surgery.

"Perhaps he fancies a cigarette," laughed the shopping bag lady. Puzzled, we all stared at the closed door.

Only a short time later, and thumb man came out, beaming with a broad smile. He waved the thumb in the air, with great pride. It was almost back to normal, the black blood behind the nail had gone.

"Doc apologised, said it was an old trick, but it always worked. He put a hot needle through the nail, and the blood gushed out. Feels great now, just got to get some plasters." He walked past me, and I had a good look at his thumbnail. Then I looked down at my ankle. Jim started shaking beside me. I turned to look at him in surprise.

"What?" I asked.

"Your face! I can tell you're wondering what the doctor is going to do to your ankle!"

CHAPTER FOURTEEN

It had only been a few moments, a painful few moments and I limped out of the surgery. The doctor had looked at it and manhandled it. "No breaks as far as I can see, a crêpe bandage, painkillers, and rest for a few days. If it doesn't improve, go and get it x-rayed. At your age you can't be too careful!" I rose, smiled my thanks, and limped out of the door, and shop.

Jim had helped me into the van. I settled back into the passenger seat, and half closed my eyes. The ankle was extremely painful. I was clutching a bottle of painkillers, and a crêpe bandage.
"That Doctor, I could have kicked him with my good leg. You know what he said to me?"
"I'll bet he said the usual, *'at your age'!* Back to your cottage Daisy, cup of tea, couple of painkillers, feet up and you'll feel so much better." Jim grinned at me and I smiled back.

I sat in a chair, Jim had expertly bandaged my ankle. Again, he showed expertise in wound treatment. Cleo sat on my lap, I had my mug of tea in my hand, and a couple of cookies and painkillers on the table beside me. The tension gradually eased out of my body. The pain gradually lessened in my ankle. Neither Jim nor I had suggested ringing the others. I knew what my reasons were. I wondered what Jim's reasons were. It wasn't long before I found out.

"Daisy, you have respected, and kept my secrets. I have kept them from you and everyone else." Jim sat in his chair, the mug of hot coffee steaming as he held it tight in both hands. He was staring into it, as if wondering what to say next. This was unlike Jim. I watched and waited. "I've respected your need for privacy. However, after this dog incident, I do feel that you owe me some sort of explanation." His grey eyes focused on mine with a direct compelling look. I had already decided to tell Jim. I too felt unable to keep my secret after calling upon his help. I doubted that I would have withstood an interrogation by him. Was that his previous spook training as well?

Stretching across Cleo, I retrieved my bag from the sofa. I took out the photocopies of the old photograph, and my birth certificate.

"Cleo knocked over and broke an old family watercolour painting when I was packing. The photo was in the back. It shows a woman holding a baby, and an older woman in front of the cottage. It had a date on the back, my birthday, and the place name."

"This cottage in the photo is where I found you today," Jim said. He held the photo and stared down intently at it.

"I got out of the van. Flora was loose when I had my sandwich but was sound asleep. I parked up the hill, away from the cottage. I thought I'd walk down for a closer look. I must have been careless, the van door wasn't properly closed. I walked a little way and stood staring at the cottage. Suddenly the front door opened, a woman and a German Shepherd came out. She set the dog onto me, and it raced up towards me barking. Flora raced to my rescue, barking at the oncoming dog." I laughed, but it turned into almost a sob, as I relived the moment. "It was terrifying, Flora would have been…"

"Okay, what happened then?" Jim hurried me on, I think he was afraid I might cry.

"The front door opened a slit, the woman whistled through it, and the dog ran back to the cottage. I grabbed Flora and turned to rush up the hill. I slipped on long wet grass and hurt my ankle. I crawled back to the van and rang you."

Jim was silent, his brow furrowed as he sat thinking. He reached for the actual photo which had been in the bag. "This photo has a name and address on the back of the photographer. He can be contacted for more information. What's the significance of the birth certificate?"

"The name on the birth certificate is mine, but the mothers name is not the one who brought me up. My parents always said I was born in Bristol, but we never had my birth certificate, it had been lost. This birth certificate shows that I was born in Wisteria cottage, on Bodmin Moor!"

"What about legal forms and such, how did your parents manage?"

"I don't really know. We moved around such

a lot when I was young. Certificates were always lost in the post or on the move. Do you think that woman recognised me? She looked familiar to me, I don't know why. I've never seen her before, but I seem to have known her forever. Perhaps she recognised me, that's why she set the dog on me!"

"Calm down Daisy," said Jim. He wasn't looking at me. It had been said automatically. He was thinking hard.

If only I hadn't hurt my ankle. All I wanted to do was pace up and down. I realised that my hands were twisting over and over, just like a heroine in Victorian melodrama. Jim put his hand over them and looked at me. "Okay I'm calming down. It's ..." A few deep breaths, and I relaxed against the cushions.

"You've been dwelling on this for a long time. Alone with your thoughts it's become..." Jim paused.

"An obsession?" I finished for him.

Jim laughed. "Verging on it! Let's work on the problem together. It'll be easier on you. Could you bear to have the others involved? I should imagine Demelza and Maggie may have local knowledge that might help."

I drank my tea and thought carefully. To hug this secret to myself had been my immediate concern. Why? I wondered if my...

"Daisy, stop analysing everything. We can all help you. Even if we can't, you have shared your problem. You do bottle everything up."

"Yes, you're right. Today would have been easier if I'd had someone with me," I acknowledged.

Jim reached for his phone, "I'll call the others."

Did I want the others involved? Why wouldn't I want their involvement? Was it a fear that a shameful secret would emerge? Perhaps if they knew of my horrible ancestors and family, they wouldn't like me? Again, that persistent fear of not being liked, of not being part of the group. That had always been my problem. I had dressed conservatively, eager to blend in. I tried to please everyone, especially Nigel, and where had it got me?

"They're on their way and they have news." Jim put his phone away with a satisfied air. He was just like a maestro conducting an orchestra, getting the musicians in their places.

Flora barked excitedly to see me when she came in with Martin. My cottage seemed suddenly full of people. After my ankle was inspected, my story was told and explained to the others.

"Daisy, I know that cottage, it's the one down by the old bridge, isn't it?" Maggie said.

"Yes, Wisteria cottage, just above the bridge."

Maggie continued, "Violet Trethowan lives there with Sheba. She's a lovely lady, very quiet and reserved. We are in the church choir, and the WI together. I can't believe she could set Sheba onto you. And I can't imagine Sheba would hurt you. Why did you want to look at that cottage?"

Jim answered before I could think of a reply. I still felt shy about the birth certificate. Somehow Jim had realised this and spoke for me. "There's a possibility that Daisy might be related to her in some way."

"Demelza was right all along. You are family. She will be so thrilled," Sheila clapped her hands delightedly.

Maggie stared at me. Really stared at me. I felt so self-conscious and was sure that I was reddening. "What? What is it Maggie?"

"Do you know, that apart from your hair and clothes you look very much like Violet. There is a strong family resemblance. Demelza was right, you are related to her." Maggie said.

"What was your news?" Jim asked. He realised I was becoming distressed about this probing into my history, so he adroitly changed the subject.

"I found out from the back history of puppies for sale, about a pet shop. It's in a village the other side of the moor. It's a farmhouse up a lane. They sell dog and cat food, but their main selling point is that they deliver the food. Every month a couple of puppies seem to come up for sale. There's two puppies for sale today, a couple of dachshund puppies." Sheila said.

"I think a visit to look..." began Jim.

"No!" Maggie exclaimed. "It's fatal Jim, you'll bring them home," said Maggie. I nodded agreement.

"I'm not going, I know I'd buy the lot," said

Sheila.

"I'm not going either," agreed Martin.

"Well, I'm going, and I have to hurry to get there before they close. Who's coming with me?" Jim said.

"I'll go," said Maggie. "And I'll make sure we don't return with any more pups!"

CHAPTER FIFTEEN

Maggie set off with Jim. She called out of the car window to us.

"Don't worry, we won't bring any more dogs home!"

I looked at the others. "We have four dogs already, what are we going to do with Maisie and her pups?" I asked. Sheila and Martin didn't seem to know what to say.

"We'll just have to see," said Sheila.

Martin went back to the library and his computers. He was investigating the Davies land and farmhouse on the Internet. Sheila decided to join him with her iPad, searching for further puppy sales over the last few months. I joined them in the library and began searching online ancient maps of the area. That puppy farm had to be somewhere. It seemed impossible that the RSPCA and the police had searched the land and farmhouse with no success. They had found nothing. Reports of dogs barking had been noted, even the vet said he had heard them, but still they hadn't been traced.

Cornwall has caves. Cornwall has minerals, valuable minerals. The empty deserted moors were once alive with men, machinery and the constant noise emanating from tin mines. I was fortunate. Blogs and websites have sprung up, run by enthusiastic amateurs. I had no interest at all in wood turning, or Dorset button making. Cornwall has sites devoted to its land and culture. There were many references to smugglers, and to Jamaica Inn on Bodmin Moor. Early miners had gone into caves and rock formations, not the usual shaft mines. These were dug straight into the hillside. Before I knew it I was involved in the type of minerals sought, and the type of rock that contained them. It was boring, but I felt it could lead to the finding of the puppy farm.

"Why am I searching this stuff on the Internet? Gerald is the one to ask. I know he's working with Jim on the old maps and information on the area, concerning the Knights Templars. But I think he ought to research where the old mine shafts, and the early miners worked into the hillside. I'll ask Jim to see if he and Gerald can look into that aspect of research," I said.

"They're taking a long time," Sheila said looking at her watch. "I wonder…" Her voice tailed away and she looked at me.

"You don't think, they were only going to have a quick look, weren't they?" I replied.

Half-an-hour later, the SUV drove into the courtyard. There was silence. "Come on Daisy, Martin. I think we ought to go and see! Maggie and Jim are very quiet out there," Sheila said.

Jim and Maggie stood together beside the SUV. Jim carried a large cardboard box. Maggie stood looking down into it. Neither looked up as we approached them.

"Okay! How many did you buy?" Sheila

demanded. She stood with one hand on her hip. She would have had both hands on hips, but she needed one for her stick

It was Maggie who spoke first. "We had to! We walked away, honestly we did. We got back in the SUV. But we just sat there. Then..." She turned and looked at Jim.

"Maggie's right. We did leave or were about to. The place was filthy. They were housed in a rabbit cage beside hamsters and guinea pigs. I don't even know how healthy they are. We had to go back in and buy them."

Sheila, Martin, and I looked into the box. Some rough straw was in the bottom on top of old newspapers. The tiny brown creatures stared up at us with huge eyes.

"Oh, my goodness, poor little things. They are in a dreadful state," said Sheila.

"I rang the vet and I got an immediate appointment. We've come back for the dog cage. And will keep them in the SUV, don't want them near the others until the vet gives them the all clear." Jim said. The dog cage was placed in the SUV, with fresh bedding. The two tiny dachshunds were placed on the bedding.

Jim and I went to the vet. Maggie and Martin remained behind to prepare a place for our new arrivals and a meal. I limped in with one of Sheila's sticks.

"What have you guys got now?" The same young redhaired vet, who had checked over Maisie and her pups greeted us with a smile.

Jim explained where he had got them from.

"Damn puppy farm! That guy at the pet shop is very clever, he never has more than the odd couple to sell. He's careful that way. Now let's look at these little ones." He lifted out the two pups. They were so tiny, almost like little rats I thought. "Malnourished, taken away from mum far too early. But they're not in a bad condition. I'll give you some puppy milk replacer, and puppy food. They'll need more of course, and there will be a schedule with the puppy milk. Bring them back in a couple of weeks." He ushered us to the door, opening it for Jim with the box. "Are you going to keep these as well?" The vet laughed at our faces.

We walked down the corridor, not daring to look at each other. It was a silent journey on the way back.

"I'll look after them in my apartment, I don't sleep much at night. Old age and my complaint keeps me awake a lot of the time. So, it's no hardship to feed these little ones through the night." Sheila met us with a beaming smile. Maggie and Sheila had prepared her apartment for the new arrivals whilst we had been to the vets. Sheila led the way to her apartment. It was in the old part of the Priory House, on the ground floor. Newly decorated, it had a wet room, waist high plugs, and widened doorways if she needed to use her wheelchair, all subject to listed building status of course.

"Martin went to the supermarket in Bodmin. It doesn't close till late. He's getting the list of extra puppy food and milk, that you phoned from the vet. He will be back any time soon." Just then her phone rang. "Martin says do we want any takeaways? Pizza or Chinese?"

"Thank goodness for Martin! I haven't started preparing the evening meal. My time has been taken up with sorting out the puppy stuff with Sheila," said Maggie.

A chorus of pizza requests was our replies. The kitchen chair had never felt more uncomfortable to me. My sprained ankle was throbbing and very painful. I shouldn't have gone to the vets with Jim, but I was the only one available at the time.

"That trip to the vet, has made your ankle worse," said Jim.

"Especially at your age," said Sheila and I in unison.

We had left the new puppies curled up fast asleep after their puppy milk. The vet had given us an immediate supply. So, we sat in the kitchen and waited for Martin to arrive with the pizzas.

"Let's eat these while they're hot," Martin said as he rushed in from the courtyard and dumped the boxes on the counter. "The other stuff can wait in the SUV until we've eaten. I'm starving!"

Halfway through our pizzas, the house phone rang. This was connected to the main Priory. Individually, we all had our mobile phones. As Martin was the nearest, he got up to answer it.

"Hello, I see. You don't have her private phone number. I'm sorry, we don't hand out residents private numbers. Who did you want to speak to? Daisy Dunwoody? And who is calling?" Martin turned towards me, a questioning look towards me. I waited to see who the caller was. Martin's face froze as he listened to the answer. "Okay, Nigel Dunwoody, her husband."

CHAPTER SIXTEEN

"Ex!" I spluttered. Waving my hands frantically at Martin, I hissed at him. "No! No!"

"If I see her, I'll tell her that you called. Oh, okay, yes I have a paper and pen. I'll write the number down. Any other message for her? Yes, you'd like to catch up with her. Goodbye Mr. Dunwoody."

"The Floozy has dumped him, that's what's happened. You mark my words!" Sheila exclaimed.

By this time, everyone knew of Nigel, of how my ex-husband had moved in with a younger woman. It had been Jake, our son, who disgusted by his father, christened the other woman, 'the Floozy'.

"What are you going to do Daisy? Or shouldn't I ask?" Maggie said, looking worried that she'd spoken out of turn.

"Nothing. I don't want to see or speak to him. I've made my new life, and there is no room in it for him. Even just to catch up!" I sat and simmered. Automatically, I munched my way through my pizza. No, Nigel was not going to turn my new life upside down. Nods of agreement, and murmurs of support had greeted my reply. I smiled at them. These were my new friends, and my support in this different lifestyle we had all embarked on. A warm feeling enveloped me, and I felt close to tears in their loving acceptance of me.

Next morning, Gerald arrived with a battered suitcase. He walked into the library nervously. Charts, maps, pamphlets, and books were bursting out of it.

"I'm so pleased to be helping you Daisy. That unpleasantness is all behind us now, isn't it?" The anxious demeanour on his face, and his eagerness to obtain my forgiveness made it impossible to refuse. It would have been like kicking an eager little kitten.

"Of course, it is Gerald. We'll forget the past and make a fresh start on our research".

"Goody! Jolly good!" He said and rubbed his hands in glee. Gerald was extremely shy and nervous. I realised that his mannerisms were a façade behind which he hid his shyness. That was something I could relate to. At that moment, any lingering resentment I felt for him disappeared.

"Gerald, good to see you. Let's see those maps of yours. Perhaps we will find where that wretched man has been hiding those poor dogs." Jim greeted Gerald as if he was a long lost friend, not our former enemy, as he led him into the library. Jim and Gerald soon became immersed in all their books and maps.

I left them to it. Martin had walked Flora for me, and they both had returned to the kitchen. Immediately they had raced in to see Maisie and her pups. I think Martin was just as keen to see them as Flora.

"Come on Flora, there are even more puppies in Sheila's apartment," I told her.

Sitting back on her haunches, she stared at me solemnly from beneath her floppy mop head. "More puppies!" At once, she pranced towards me, and we both went to Sheila's apartment.

"Come in, my grandkids came up last night to help me with them." No longer did the puppies have a cardboard box with straw for their bed. A newly decorated cardboard box had been draped with fleeces. Two fluffy type puppy toys sat in a corner, and a large sign had been painted on top of the box proclaiming, "The Dachshund Palace." A child's wooden playpen of considerable antiquity kept the pups neatly corralled.

"They fed them and played with them before they went home to bed. This morning they came before school. Their mum has always said no dogs, but even she has fallen in love with these two little ones. I'm hopeful they may have found a home." Sheila said with a laugh. I smiled back at her in relief. When fully fit and able to be moved they would have a good home. I was especially relieved that it wouldn't be my home! The puppies were fed again and fell asleep. Sheila and I, along with Flora returned to the kitchen. Flora didn't like the dachshunds. They were boring, too small, and not bouncy like Maisie's pups.

"It's nearly time to go," said Jim. "The sale you've heard about at puppy class, takes place soon at Blisland Green. Who's coming with me to watch what happens?" Maggie was too busy. Sheila said she'd stay with the pups, but I'd noticed the strain around her eyes. She'd done too much yesterday sorting things out for the pups. Sheila needed rest today, looking after the pups gave her the ideal excuse. Martin was involved with Gerald, their maps and charts and pamphlets. They were now using them, and satellite aerial maps of the area.

Blisland Green, was unusual in Cornwall with its green open space. The cottages clustered around were overshadowed by the pub and the church. The pub was a focal point on the green and the village country community life over which it presided. I joined Jim. We parked across the green and had a good view of the proposed meeting. Jim had produced a camera with a telephoto lens. Of course, he had it handy! It gave him not only an enhanced view, but photos for our later perusal. We had already been told by Martin, the colour and make of the car to look out for.

"Here she comes," said Jim. The red Honda jazz drove slowly until it reached the prearranged spot to park. A few moments later a white van arrived and parked behind her. "Look at the number plates," said Jim, with a grim look on his face.

I stared at first, unable to comprehend what he meant. "Oh, of course! They are covered in mud, they are unreadable."

"Clever," said Jim.

The car door opened, a woman and a young, excited girl got out. An elderly woman got out of the white van and walked towards them smiling.

"Another Alice!" I gasped.

"Yes, the kindly elderly woman who instils trust in the customer. Here we go, she's opening the van doors."

The three had walked round to the back of the van. The van door wouldn't open, so she called out to the driver. The driver's door opened and a man got out. He smiled at the woman and child and unlocked the door. Reaching in, he pulled out a smart basket with a puppy inside. The oohs and aahs as the puppy was exclaimed over could be heard all across the green. A conversation ensued with the elderly woman searching in the dog basket, her bag and even her jacket pockets.

"Oh dear, she's forgotten the papers," said Jim with sarcasm.

The child was given the puppy, not in the smart basket, but in another cardboard one. The money, cash I noticed, was handed over. A couple of tins of puppy food were given with a great flourish to the little girl. They went back to their car. The elderly woman, Alice number two, went round to the passenger seat of the van. The man pushed the posh basket into the van and locked and closed the door.

"What should we do? Warn the woman? Tell somebody? We can't just stand by and do nothing," I asked Jim.

"Nothing to be done. It was a private transaction. We shouldn't even be watching, we can't interfere. I don't like it. But we are powerless to do anything."

As the man locked the van door, he straightened up, and looked around the green.

"It's Ferret Face, the man from the pub," I said.

"And he spotted us!" Jim exclaimed.

Sure enough, his gaze had locked onto us. He stood still for a moment. From where I sat, I could sense the fury that engulfed him at the sight of us. One last look at us, a look that promised vengeance, and he walked round to the driver's side, got in and drove away.

CHAPTER SEVENTEEN

That night over our evening meal, it was agreed that extra care should be taken by all of us. Ferret Face was someone to be wary of.

"Always keep together. Always leave a note of where you are going, and what time you expect to be back. Phones must be charged at all times." Jim announced this in solemn tones. The cheerful atmosphere in the kitchen vanished at these words. An atmosphere descended upon us, not fear exactly but an uneasiness.

"What do you expect him to do?" A worried Martin asked Jim, stroking his beard in an agitated manner, the frown deepening on his thin face.

"I don't know, maybe nothing. I'd like us to be prepared and on our guard." We all murmured assent. It had been Jim whose foresight had saved us all from going over the cliff. We all knew that Jim's instincts or gut feelings had to be taken seriously.

"Could I get a gun? I'd love to have a weapon of some sort!" Sheila said.

"No gun!" was a universal cry from every one of us.

"I've got a can of red dye spray. Why don't you have one of those? Would you like an electronic alarm device?" Maggie asked.

"Ha, a gun would be much better," snorted a disappointed Sheila. "But they'll do."

"Daisy and I are going to the photographer

tomorrow morning. I found out that the guy who took her family photo has retired near Camelford. I phoned him this afternoon, and he's agreed to see us tomorrow morning," said Jim. Everyone stared at Jim and then at me. "Okay Daisy, I know I asked without your say-so but I knew you'd put it off. It's arranged for you to see him tomorrow morning with the photo. He's an old boy, obviously got time on his hands, and looking forward to a chat about the good old days." Jim lifted up his phone and held it towards me. "If you don't want to go, I'll ring him now and cancel. It's up to you Daisy."

All eyes turned to me, and then to Jim. Just like Wimbledon I thought, waiting for the next backhand.

"Okay, okay, we'll go! You've been..." Words failed me. I saw the truth of what Jim had said. "Yes, I was putting it off. Okay Jim. Thank you very much. We'll go." Admittedly this was said with bad grace. I was still peeved at his high-handed attitude. But I had to admit that he had been correct, and I had been scared to make the appointment and go.

"First thing in the morning we'll chat over breakfast and discuss the next steps in the investigation." Jim said as we all rose.

"Goody! Breakfast power meeting! We need an agenda and," began Sheila.

"Wait Sheila, wait until the morning. We'll discuss it then when we're all fresh." Maggie smiled at the enthusiastic octogenarian.

I took the dog and cat into my courtyard

garden before bed. Then I made a bedtime drink for myself. Opening my emails, I found one from Jake. There were photographs of him and Lisa holding gold nuggets! They were very small, like crumbs, and looked infinitesimal in Jake's large hand. Dirty and unkempt, they both looked delighted with their find. Australia has certainly delivered everything they went for, I thought sadly. I was delighted for them, but unhappy at the thought of them being across the world from me. I read again the hardships they were enduring in the trials of outback life. Excitement in actually finding gold could be felt even through an email.

Then the tone changed. *"Sorry Mum but have to tell you that Dad contacted me. He wanted to catch up with me, first time for years! But he really wanted to find out how he could contact you. I wouldn't give him your number or address. But I reckon he will get it from Elsie. Something must have gone wrong with him. I expect he's been dumped. Look out for yourself Mum. You've got a great new life with friends. Ignore him, because I'm going to. He's never been interested in me, it was always his work and his girlfriends, don't get trapped again in that dull boring life."*

The milky drink had congealed by the time I reached for it. An unpleasant skin floated on the top. I poured it down the sink. I opened the cupboard and got out a glass and the whisky bottle. Then, I put them back. Was I going to get in a state because of Nigel? I put the kettle on. But I did reach for the cookie tin. My resolutions could only be taken so far! Tomorrow I had a breakfast meeting, correction, breakfast power meeting! Smiling to myself, I went to bed with my mug of tea, cookie and thought of my new friends and the Priory. No way was Nigel ever going to upset me again.

The breakfast meeting in the Priory was quite surreal. It was quite strange in that Sheila's excitement turned it almost into a party. Aches and pains were forgotten as she awaited new instructions for her part in the action. I smiled to myself, as I saw the number and variety of pills that we took at breakfast time. Not one of us admitted to getting old, but those pills and packets told a different story!

"The delivery man is coming with dog food supplies. Can you deal with him Maggie or Sheila?" Martin asked. "Gerald will be here soon, and he and I are going to check out the satellite photos against the old maps of the Priory. If you need us to help with anything, just give us a shout."

"I'm going with Daisy to meet up with the old photographer," said Jim. I smiled weakly at everybody, the sleepless night had increased my fears. What would I discover? Would it be better just to leave it alone? The past was buried. Shall I? Should I? My thoughts ran around my head in an endless circle.

"We all agree that you need to sort out this family business Daisy. The investigation can wait for a day whilst you go with Jim. We have no other leads to follow anyway." Maggie stood leaning against the sink, her arms on her hips and glared at me. The others all nodded solemnly and agreed, all looking at me with determination. Their mock anger made me smile.

"All right," I spread out my hands and capitulated. "If I find out that I'm related to an axe murderer or some other kind of horrid villain, I'll blame you lot!" There was good-natured laughter and sympathy for me, as we all rose from the breakfast table. We left our power breakfast to begin our day.

The small cottage was on the brow of a hill not far from Camelford. The garden was neat and tidy, and it would be a colourful picture in spring and summer. Slowly I opened the car door. I wasn't nervous. I was frightened. Should I leave? What if this knowledge changes not only my life but Jake's for the worse. What if...

"Stop it Daisy! Come on get out of that car. If you can fire a gun at a villain, you can cope with whatever knowledge awaits you. You are you, your son Jake is Jake. Nothing you can learn can possibly change either of you. He is a positive young man with his own identity. There is nothing that you can find out now that would change that."

I got out of the car. Jim's words had not been said with conviction. He hadn't looked at me. We both knew it would change me and my outlook on life. But I was grateful that he'd said them. I walked up the path and took a deep breath as I rang the doorbell.

"Coming, coming," the voice was surprisingly youthful, as was its owner who opened the door to us.

The photograph was in my hand, as I stood on the doorstep. I was going to let Jim do the talking. I was too jittery to attempt it. The old man ignored Jim, he focused immediately on the photograph. Gently he took it from my hands. Then he stared intently at me.

"There's no mistake. You are one of them, no doubt about it. The image of your mother at that age. The Trethowans have strong genes in their family. Always some family resemblance in each and every one of them."

"Is there?" I asked. We followed him into a cheerful sitting room. Sunlight streamed through the window, and the false gas log fire gave the room a welcoming warmth. He led the way through the sitting room to the kitchen. Teacups, milk and sugar bowl, and a plate of biscuits, were set out upon the checked tablecloth. Again, my words wouldn't come. I didn't know what to say. How to phrase it? Where would I start?

Jim came to my rescue again. I could see that he was enjoying it, too much so. Once out of here, I would get my confidence back. I had to.

"Daisy only found this photo recently. Can you tell us more about the people in the photograph?" Walter, the photographer was filling the kettle and had his back to us. We had to wait while the kettle boiled. He poured the boiling water into the teapot, and then we had to wait for it to brew. Jim's impatience wore out. "Do you know any of them? Can you tell us anything at all about them?" Jim persisted.

The old man poured out the tea, handing us both a cup. After proffering the sugar to both of us, he stirred in three teaspoons to his own cup.

"Know them? Of course, I do!"

CHAPTER EIGHTEEN

We waited. He stirred his tea thoroughly. Then he reached for a biscuit. A sip of tea, a crunch of the biscuit and he gave a satisfied sigh of pleasure. The teacup was placed onto his saucer.

I moved restlessly on the hard kitchen chair. My bag was in my hand before I knew it, and I was standing.

"Sit down Daisy," Jim said. He grabbed my arm and gently pushed me back onto my chair. "We are here now, wait and see what he has to say," he whispered.

The old man had been staring down at his plate and was oblivious of my actions. At the mention of my name however, he raised his head and looked at me. "Daisy that was it. And your twin sister was called Violet!" He gave me a beaming smile at this feat of memory.

"I'm a twin?" I exclaimed. "I was told that I after I was born my parents died shortly afterwards in a car crash. There was never any mention of a twin sister," I stammered out, gazing at the man wildly, my head in an absolute whirl.

Now it was Walter's turn to gasp. "Told your parents were dead after you were born? That's a terrible lie! Your mother is still alive!"

The kitchen was old-fashioned. It had blue and white crockery on an old dresser, faded gingham curtains in matching blue, and a checked tablecloth, with coordinating tea towels. My mind started cataloguing the old man's kitchen decor and the many objects in it. My mind had escaped from his words. It didn't want to come back, it didn't want to acknowledge the realisation of those words. I noted even Walter had been shocked my astonishment.

"Daisy's mother is still alive? But how? Where?" Jim's words were uttered for me. But I could see by his face that he was stunned as I was.

Walter went quiet, he spoke softly as if he had drifted back into the past. "It seems a long time ago, and it was a different age. Different times then when your mother became pregnant. In those days no girl could bring up a baby out of wedlock, never mind two of them." He took another sip of his tea and shook his head, still intent at the beginning of the story, and determined to tell it his way. "Your mother and her mother, that would be your grandmother, said that your Gran had given birth to a late baby. Unexpected like. Somehow you were smuggled to your aunt who couldn't have children. The aunt who took you promised to keep in touch and visit often. Your mother and grandmother wanted the two girls to grow up friends, even though they were really twins."

"So, what happened?" Jim asked.

"One day the aunt and her husband had gone, no notion of where they went. Took you with them. Your mother and grandmother were heartbroken. They tried to find you, but it was

111

hopeless," Walter replied.

"We moved around a lot when I was younger. Mum and Dad were always scared of forms, and always tried never to fill them in. They always said they'd lost my birth certificate. That must be why," I said thoughtfully, the words came out automatically. But I had difficulty in saying them. My mind was still trying to adjust to the news I had been given.

Jim pushed my cup of tea towards me. "Drink this Daisy, you've had one hell of a shock."

"That you have love." Walter looked at me and rose to his feet. He went to a cupboard and brought back a glass and a bottle of brandy. Pouring out a small tot he put into my shaking hand. "Drink it love. Never would I have told it blunt like that if only I'd realised. I thought you must've known. Your mother is still alive, she's in a care home near St Austell." I stared down at the glass in my hand. I normally don't drink. I don't like alcohol, or its effect on me. Jim pushed the glass towards me and nodded. I realised that I was absolutely shattered by this news, and in shock. Gingerly I took a sip. The burning hot liquid seemed to warm my whole body. I took another sip. Yes, I felt better, but that was enough. Two sips only for me. I put the glass down on the table. Walter looked at it, "had enough?" At my definite nod, he upended the rest of the brandy into his teacup.

"Do you think Daisy would be welcome if she

went to visit her mother and her sister?" Jim asked the question that had been at the forefront of my mind. And yet, what if this proposed meeting didn't go well. Not every reunited family had a happy ending. I'd heard of some disastrous stories.

"Of course, they would! I'm delighted to meet you. You're a cousin of mine and of Demelza's. She always said you were family. You go to Demelza, best you go to her. She'll sort it all out with you, and your mother and sister. That's it, best go to Demelza."

Goodbyes were said and I was sitting in the car as we drove back to the Priory. My head was whirling. Was it the brandy? I don't drink, so maybe that's what affected me, especially at ten o'clock in the morning. Or was it the startling news? I was a twin! I had a mother who was still alive! And living in a care home near St Austell. "She must be old," I said.

Jim knew exactly what I meant. "She must be in her nineties, she may not remember much. Perhaps Demelza will be able to tell you how fit and well she is now. Demelza will have all the information for you."

"And won't Demelza just love that! Demelza was right after all, I am her cousin!" I laughed, but it wasn't a proper laugh. I was struggling not to cry. I mustn't cry. Once I started, I wouldn't stop. A text message had me reaching for my bag. "It's Sheila. She says can we get back quickly, they think they have a lead. I don't know if I can face them yet. I don't know what to tell them."

The car engine ticked as the heat dissipated in the still frosty air, as we sat in the courtyard. Jim's hand gave mine a squeeze. "You don't want to tell them just yet do you? Why don't you wait until we see Demelza. We can discuss it with Demelza tomorrow and get the full story. Then we can tell the others. You will feel more like it then. There's no hurry." He smiled at me as he got out of the car. "Come on Daisy! Sheila will burst with her news if we keep her waiting any longer." I wiped away the tears. Managing a weak smile, I got out of the car.

We went into the library. "Look, look! Come and look." Sheila was standing by the table and pointed to the map. "Look there. See that track leading nowhere, just going on up into the moor. It's well used, you can see that by the well -worn tracks on it, but then it comes to a sudden stop. We all thought that seemed very fishy, so we looked on the satellite pictures. They show the same thing. A well-worn track leading towards a hillside, then nothing!"

"I brought a very old Cornish map of ancient mine workings. It shows that this track leads up to a ridge in the hillside, almost a cliff face. This information is not on any other maps, only on this old one." Gerald said, his face alight with enthusiasm and immense satisfaction that he had provided so much help to the investigation.

"But it's not any old mine!" exclaimed Sheila. The excitement was evident in her voice, her broad grin, and as always, those bouncing curls. "No! It's not any old mine working. This old map shows that this was a mine for gold. It's a gold mine!"

"Gold!" Jim breathed. "That would explain it. The murders, the violent actions taken to keep us from nosing around. I never could understand why anyone would murder over a few puppies. But gold is at an all-time high price. Pure gold is certainly worth mining for. If there's enough gold there, it's worth killing for!"

CHAPTER NINETEEN

"The puppy farming is definitely not their main business. Just a way of making money and giving a false impression of the mine workings going on there. But that's not their main business at all, it must be the search for gold," declared Maggie.

"When do we take action? We must do something about it." Sheila looked round at us.

"Further research and more reconnaissance of the area is needed," said Jim.

"But I thought we could just go down there and..." Sheila almost wailed.

Jim stared at Sheila, not unkindly he said. "How can we? It's private property. What if we find nothing? We have to be certain as to where it is, and what it consists of. Then we call in the police. Not before!"

Sheila subsided like a defeated balloon. She'd been so enthusiastic. At a single word from Jim, Sheila would have marched down the valley and demanded to see the puppy farm.

"Jim is right. We must be certain, otherwise he would just carry on or move elsewhere. We must get enough evidence for the authorities to act," Martin said.

"This gold business places a new perspective on everything. It explains why they are becoming ruthless in keeping it secret. They murdered Alice and tried to kill us. Any more investigations we do, must be done with extreme secrecy and caution. Our very lives depend on it," said Jim.

"Do we tell Tenby what we have discovered?" Martin asked.

"Tell him what. We have discovered an old map, and there is a possibility of a gold mine on Davies land. Tenby would laugh in our faces." Jim replied and shook his head.

It was puppy class time. Again! Martin could face it as long as Maggie was with him. They came to the cottage twenty minutes before they needed to leave. Flora had to be brushed. She had to look her best for her outing. Maggie insisted on it. But Flora did not realise the importance of looking her puppy best. Ten minutes passed. Cleo and I sat on the window seat, side-by-side, and watched the show. Cleo had on her snarky look, disgust mixed with horror. I sat back and enjoyed watching two adults crawl around my floor. First, Flora grabbed the brush. Over the sofa, under the table she raced. She was grinning! I didn't know how she managed it. There was definitely a puppy grin on her face, despite her teeth being firmly clamped on the brush.

Satisfied with their efforts to make Flora presentable, Maggie and Martin sat on the sofa. Both took a deep breath, and Maggie reached for the puppy harness. The twenty minutes were up. Flora was settled into her cage in the back of the SUV, and an exhausted pair waved goodbye. And they still had puppy class to get through.

"Rather them than me," I told Cleo as I went back into the cottage.

I cleaned the kitchen. I did my laundry. I cleaned the whole of the upstairs and was just vacuuming the lounge when my doorbell rang. Jim stood there. He glanced past me at the vacuum and sniffed.

"Housework? Cleaning? You hate it. You always do it at night to get it over with before the next day."

"Coffee?" I stood back and waved him in.

"Yes please. I'll make it. You put that vacuum away, and all those cleaning materials back in the cupboard."

I put the vacuum away, the feather duster, and the various cloths I had out. That had been some cleaning binge that I had embarked upon. I was grateful for the mug of tea Jim handed me.

"Come on Daisy. You can't bottle everything up. I understood yesterday when you wanted to think things over before speaking to the others. But you've slept on it. What are you going to do? Firstly, about your ex-husband, and then about your sister and mother."

We stood in the kitchen. Cleo was wandering around the back garden. For a time, I watched her. Another sip of tea, and I placed the mug down on the counter. Jim leant back, his arms folded and looked at me. Not his sneering look, but a kindly compassionate one. He waited for me to verbalise my thoughts. There was no hurry. For that I was grateful. All night my mind had jumped about. I didn't know what to think. Was I happy at the news? Sad at the lost wasted years without my true family? No, I was scared. Terrified at what at my advanced age, I was embarking upon. Jim's words that my discoveries couldn't change Jake or myself had been wrong. I had been changed in a matter of moments, I had a sister, a twin sister, and a mother. Jake now had an aunt and grandmother. There had been snatches of sleep. Dreams and half remembered memories had seemed to merge into a whirling kaleidoscope. At three in the morning, I'd given up and settled on the sofa to watch TV. My neck still ached after my lopsided slumber. No decisions had been made. That was why I embarked on my cleaning spree. Cleaning meant that I didn't think. I was concentrating on something else.

"You didn't get much sleep." It was a statement from Jim, not a question.

"No, I ended up on the sofa. My neck keeps reminding me."

"Any nearer a decision after your sleepless night, and your cleaning jag?"

"I'd have said no a few minutes ago," I finished my tea, placing it down on the countertop. "It was when I was watching Cleo in the garden that everything became clear to me."

"Cleo?" Jim was puzzled and stared out of the window at my cat.

Lifting each paw, one after the other, in

distaste she wandered over the wet grass. As if she knew we were talking about her, she looked back towards the kitchen window. I waved at her. She seemed to acknowledge my wave with a dip of her head, and then resumed her investigations. Jim watched me but he said nothing. He wasn't even smiling at my actions.

"So, Cleo...?"

"I love my cat. This cottage suits both of us. Nigel hates cats. He hated Cornwall especially the open moorland."

"So, because you love your cat..." Jim began.

I waved him into silence. "My cottage here, my cat here, are all mine. It's my world. My new world, and I love it. Nigel wanted his life his way. For a quiet peaceful family routine, I gave in to him. It's not even about his unfaithfulness, unforgivable as it is. My life at this very late stage, has to be lived my way. I know Nigel, he manoeuvred things to suit him and..." I spread my hands out, at a loss of how to explain my ex-husband and his manipulations.

"No Daisy, not now. I doubt he could change you or shift you from any purpose you set your mind on now." Nursing the warm coffee mug between his fingers, Jim paused and taking great care over his next words he continued. "Is it the Priory? Or is it the dangers we've experienced together? Or has our crazy group of misfits, of different backgrounds and ages bonded together, and in so doing altered all our outlooks on life? I know I've changed. So has Martin, and so have you. I think Maggie has to some extent."

"Sheila?" I asked.

"No! Not Sheila! She was, and always will be just Sheila," was his reply.

We laughed and smiled together. It felt good. Someone who let you think for yourself, be yourself, and in American type talk, always had your back.

"Nigel will get a polite no. I don't want any contact at all with him. As for my new family that I have discovered," I paused while I took a breath trying to formulate my thoughts into words. "I'll go and see Demelza at her house. Away from the Priory. After that conversation, I'll talk to the others about the discoveries I've made, and my twin sister and mother."

"Great. You've made your own decisions and I think that they are sensible ones. Do you want me to take you to see Demelza? I'll wait in the car, or come in with you, or you can go in alone. Your decision Daisy."

"I'd like you to take me Jim. I'd like you to come in with me please, I might get flustered and won't be able to explain everything properly. If I do, I know you'll clarify the situation."

Jim nodded, raised his coffee cup in salute to me and smiled. "I think that's a sensible decision, we'll see what Demelza has to say..." He stopped talking and turning to the front window said. "I thought I heard the SUV a few minutes ago. Why they both just sitting there? Oh no! Martin and Flora haven't been expelled from the puppy class again."

I joined him at the window. "I don't know. They've got out, and both are talking, but they don't look so happy. They are opening up the boot and getting Flora out."

"I'm going to see what's wrong," Jim walked to the front door and opened it.

CHAPTER TWENTY

Maggie and Martin whirled around as they heard us approach the SUV. Both turned to look at each other. Guilty looks passed between them.

"You tell them," muttered Martin.

"No! You offered," said Maggie.

Jim and I stood uncertain as to what we were about to be told. I wasn't sure that I wanted to know what it was all about. Those guilty looks meant trouble. No more trouble please, I thought.

It was Maggie who stepped forward. "You remember us telling you about the dachshund puppy bought by the woman in a layby? She was at our last puppy class with her dachshund Lottie."

"Yes," said Jim. That word was slow and wary and held a depth of meaning.

I rolled my eyes, I knew what was coming. But a small hopeful part of me pleaded to be wrong.

"She brought it today. She doesn't want it anymore. Each year she has a litter from her dogs, but definitely not puppy farming. They only ever have two or three litters in their lifetime. But Lottie has no papers. They were promised but never came. The phone is always dead, discontinued, and she can't find the people that sold Lottie to her." Maggie paused for breath and looked at us.

It was Martin who continued, "it's only

worth her while if these are pedigree pups, complete with papers. She also needs the grandparents and kennels named in the family tree, and..."

Jim exploded. "You brought another flipping pup home! How many are we going to have? How many more dogs will we have, before we have as many as the wretched puppy farm?"

It was probably not the most diplomatic thing to do. In fact, it added fuel to Jim's fire. But I couldn't help it. Afterwards, I realised that it was a massive relief from the tension that had built up in me for some time. I leant against the SUV and just shook with laughter. Jim's indignant expression made it worse. I pointed a finger at him, "as many as the wretched puppy farm." I repeated his words and laughed even more.

Maggie stared at me open mouthed. Then she looked at Jim's indignant face. Maggie giggled, snorted, and dissolved into laughter. Martin began a slow tentative smile. Jim's furious face took on a reddish hue. Martin and Maggie had now caught the giggles from me and were helpless with laughter.

"Come on Jim. There is a funny side to this," I said.

A moment later, his reluctant smile had turned into laughter.

"What's going on? What am I missing?" Sheila's voice reached us as she came out of the Priory kitchen. Ben and Rosie followed their grandma, and a younger edition of Sheila followed them. What a resemblance I thought, as Lesley joined her mother.

"Those two have come home with yet another puppy," Jim's accusing finger pointed directly at Maggie and Martin.

"Another puppy! Mummy can we?" Rosie cried out, turning an eager face to her mother.

"No! No!" Lesley, their mother almost screamed it.

I grinned at her, "I know the feeling," I said.

The cage door was opened. Flora lay curled up beside another tiny dachshund puppy.

"That's Lottie. She may be older than Hans or Fritz. I don't think she's from the same litter. She's been seen by the vet, and is perfectly healthy, just undernourished."

"Oh Mummy! She's gorgeous." Both children cooed and fussed over the puppy.

"She can join Fritz and Hans for now," Sheila said.

"We are having both boys next week. Dad has to fix the fence round the garden, so they can't get out. Then they'll come home with us and live with us for ever and ever!" Rosie said dancing around and around.

"And we are coming to puppy classes with Flora," exclaimed Ben with pride.

"That will be great, it'll be good to have you and both puppies join us," said Maggie.

"Perhaps we ought to hire a minibus to take all the Priory puppies to the class. Or shall we just book the entire lesson for the Priory dog pound?" Jim said, a sour expression on his face.

"Jim how can you? You know you love them

all as much as we do!" Sheila cried out.

He did look shamefaced at her rebuke and gave her a weak smile.

Martin opened the cage. "Let's take her in with the boys." But Lottie didn't want to go in with the boys. She liked Flora. Four tiny paws dug into the fleecy cover, and she whined a complaint. As she was taken into the Priory House, complaining yips and her wriggling could be heard and seen all the way. Flora sat watching the pup leave, a crestfallen look upon her face. She gave a tiny whimper. I pretended that I hadn't heard it.

After entering the cottage, Flora had a drink, a biscuit, and a lick from Cleo. Minutes later Flora was in her usual after puppy class position-flat on her back, all four paws in the air. I smiled down at her as I got ready for my meeting with Demelza. Jim had made the appointment for that afternoon. Demelza, he told me, had been puzzled but was far too polite to say anything, she had only agreed.

We drove in Jim's car, a smart black Audi convertible, which he loved with a passion. Totally unsuitable for Cornish lanes and the winter weather, he was still loath to sell it. The Priory SUV became his workhorse, but Maggie had needed it for today's large grocery shop.

Demelza lived in a cottage near to Bodmin. We drew up outside it and I commented upon its neat pristine appearance.

"Why don't you comment on the flowers? Or perhaps the fields behind the cottage?" Jim said. I swivelled round in my seat to stare at him. "Delaying tactics Daisy. Come on, let's get you in there and this all sorted out." His warm smile towards me meant that his words were not unkindly meant.

"Okay Jim. Let's do it." I got out of the car and walked up the path to the front door. "The flowers are not lovely at this time of year, but I bet they are spectacular when they do come out!" Determined to get the last word, my words were a feeble attempt to get control of myself, and of course Jim.

"Come in Daisy, Jim. I've got the kettle on." The door had opened before I'd reached it. Demelza stood there with a broad smile on her face for us. She looked so very different, but I couldn't work out why. When she turned to lead the way down the hall, Jim nudged me and nodded towards her feet. No white wellingtons! On her feet were huge fluffy bunny slippers.

The kitchen was bathed in sunshine. It streamed in on the cream printed curtains and tablecloth. The huge oval table had chairs around it with matching seat pads. A cream Aga blasted out a welcoming heat against the cold chill of the morning. At the far end, easy chairs looked out of doors opening onto the garden and the fields beyond.

"What a wonderful room! It's so warm and cosy," I said.

"I love it! This was my parents cottage, that

they inherited from my grandmother. It had never been touched since my grandmother's day. When I inherited it I promised myself I would redo the whole room. It was dark and dingy with an old coal stove type of fireplace and grate. That along with the antique fire implements and grandmother's old ornaments were sold, and they fetched enough money to pay for my new Aga."

"You've done a fantastic job on it, it's wonderful," agreed Jim.

"Now here's your tea Daisy. Coffee for myself and Jim, and how about one of these ginger biscuits?" She sat down at the table with us. "What's all this about then?"

Jim looked at me. I knew he thought I should speak, but he was ready to step in if I couldn't. The realisation dawned upon me, that not only should I speak, but I wanted to.

"When I was packing to come down here, Cleo..." I began and told my story. I handed Demelza photocopies of the photo that had started my search, and finally the birth certificate. I had been surprised that she hadn't spoken once during my tale. I stared at her, wondering what she was thinking.

Demelza fingered both copies. She looked from one to the other of them. Finally, she put them down on the table. A sigh escaped her lips, and she sat back and looked at me. A sorrowful gaze that puzzled me.

"I knew you were family the moment I saw you. It's the eyes and the hairline. Can't explain it. But we all have it. I thought you were a distant cousin, or something like that. But this!" She touched the birth certificate with a finger. "This is something else!" There was a moment when I swallowed hard. I stared at her, the harsh sunlight causing that zigzag scar to come into prominence on her face. I was scared of what she was going to say next. "Your Mum, she's never given up hope of finding you. She is all of ninety years old now. She's in a care home St Austell Way. Bright as a button she is, she'll be over the moon to see you."

"She will... You think she will be pleased?" My voice faded away. I found I couldn't say any more. My fingers gripped a tissue and wound it round and round until it was nothing but a damp wad.

"Of course she will! As for Violet, she will be thrilled as well."

"No, she won't! She set a dog on me," I said with feeling, and told of my visit to Wisteria cottage.

"That was you!" Demelza began to laugh. "Oh no, what a mix-up to be sure. Violet rang to tell me all about it."

"Did she?" I was taken aback by her laughter, and none too pleased about it.

"Violet thought you were the estate agent woman. She is a brash Londoner and has a buyer for Wisteria cottage. She is determined to sell it at an inflated price, because she gets a nice juicy commission! She won't leave Violet alone. She keeps pestering her. Violet refuses to wear her glasses and set Sheba onto you thinking you were the estate agent. What a laugh!"

My throbbing ankle, still swollen and painful, did not find it funny, I thought. But I smiled weakly. At least I hadn't been the actual intended victim. Another half hour passed. Demelza had brought out photo albums. I grew tired, bewildered, and confused by all the names. But it had been settled. Tomorrow morning I would go and meet Violet, and my Mother at the care home.

CHAPTER TWENTY ONE

"I'm scared," I admitted it both to myself and Jim. We had left Demelza's cottage and were on our way back to the Priory. Leaving the cottage, I was still bemused and astonished at what I had learnt about my new relations. And I was pleased with myself, because I had told the story of finding the photograph clearly to Demelza without a single stammer or flustered word.

"Bound to be. I'd be scared if I was in your shoes," replied Jim.

"Would you?" I couldn't believe he meant it. I turned to look at him in amazement, at this sign of weakness.

"Yes, I'm like you in that I have a few family members and can only cope with a few close friends."

Sitting back in the car, I thought about Jim's words and wondered. He said he had few family members, but he'd never mentioned any of them. A few close friends, I wondered who they were, and again there had been no comments about any of them. Everything I had learnt about Jim came in tiny snippets. Would I ever get to know the real Jim? Did anyone ever know Jim, the actual person? The journey back from Demelza's cottage had been a different route from our way there. Jim stopped the car outside a small pub.

"Let's have a drink here. You need to unwind before returning and talking to the others.

They will even do you a pot of tea here!"

When I finished drinking my second cup of tea, I put the cup down with a sigh. What an enlightened pub I thought, that could produce a decent pot of tea willingly. I'll make a note of this pub and return here again. It was pleasant, homely, yet sparkled with cleanliness, and the cheerful landlady obviously loved her job.

"You were right. I do feel better. Honestly Jim, out of everything that was said when we talked to Demelza, the photo albums, and her stories, only one thing sticks out."

An intent gaze sharpened Jim's features as he waited for me to continue. "Well? What really stood out?"

"Demelza was not wearing white wellingtons. She was wearing fluffy bunny slippers."

Jim's prolonged laughter ended in a coughing fit. He got no sympathy from me. "Daisy! Honestly, I can't believe it, all that life changing information that you got. New relatives galore and an unexpected mother. What do you do? You focus on Demelza's wellington boots!" At that remark, even I found it funny, sort of, and gave him a weak smile.

The journey home to the Priory, after my cup of tea helped calm me down, and I felt able to face everyone.

"Jim, Daisy come here, I've got to tell you, I have got loads of Intel!" Sheila cried out as soon as she saw us get out of the car. She was standing in the middle of the courtyard surrounded by boxes. Her face was wreathed in a broad smile, and those curls were bouncing in excitement. "I had a chat with the deliveryman, and found out lots," she said.

"Must have been a long chat, considering the number of boxes he has delivered," murmured Jim as we both edged our way past boxes in the courtyard, and along the corridor to the kitchen.

"Where are you going to put them all? You can't bring them in the kitchen. There is no room in the kitchen or in the back utility room. You've got to find somewhere else," cried out Maggie, almost wringing her hands in despair at the encroaching boxes in her kitchen.

"Don't worry, Martin and I cleared out one of the old stables. We'll use it as a temporary home for all the dog food." Gerald's voice rose over a large pile of the boxes. He charged in towards us, grabbing a couple of the boxes. A broad smile creased his owlish face, and he struggled out with the boxes with an air of importance.

Maggie watched him go and then turned towards me. "He's worked really hard. Gerald is trying to make up for all that previous unpleasantness." I nodded, what could I say? Gerald had apologised and had done everything he could. Not only to help us, but I could see he wanted to become one of us. Would he? Would Gerald turn the Priory five into the Priory six?

"What about you Daisy? Did Demelza have any more news for you?" Sheila smiled at me, and her eyes were avid with curiosity. Martin had arrived to carry out more boxes. At Sheila's question he stood still, his arms full, but he was unwilling to leave in case he missed my answer.

"Perhaps Daisy would rather leave it until another time," Jim said.

"No it's all right. You all know what I was hoping to discover. It might as well be now. I'm in shock! I discovered that I was born in Wisteria cottage! I've discovered a twin sister was also born, obviously the same time, at Wisteria cottage. And that was the woman who set her dog upon me!"

Gasps and exclamations broke out into the silence that had greeted my initial announcement. I waved my hands to silence them.

"Shush, that is a surprise. But it's not a shock. This is a shock... I always knew I was adopted but was told that my parents died in a car crash after I was born. Not true." Again, I had to wave them into silence. "This is the shock. My mother is still alive and in a care home near St Austell!"

Gerald joined us that evening. His delight at being part of our crowd was obvious, and to be truthful, he actually fitted in with our oddball mix of characters.

"Now Sheila, what did that delivery guy have to tell you?" Jim asked Sheila. "With Daisy's announcement, we never did get to hear about your Intel."

"He delivers to the Davies farmhouse. He leaves it up a track to be collected later. Sometimes he meets other delivery vans going up there and returning back down. Often it can be builders merchants, and he even saw a lorry going up with bags of cement."

"Interesting," said Jim. "Why would a puppy farm need bags of cement? Why would they be having builders merchants deliver to them?"

"Was it worth all the boxes I ordered?" Sheila teased him.

"Yes, Sheila it was well worth it," Jim gave Sheila an unusually warm smile, which he reserved solely for her.

The kitchen door opened and Tenby walked in. "Heard you lot are running a puppy farm. Is that right? Heard you cornered the market on dachshunds." His loud guffaw echoed round the large kitchen.

"Where did you hear that?" Jim asked, disconcerted at how our business was being gossiped about the area.

"Joe at the police station. His kids are in Ben's class at school. Full of excitement Ben is, at getting not just one puppy, but two. Joe's furious, he is being pestered night and day for a puppy now."

"We've got a spare dachshund," several voices spoke at once.

Tenby laughed when he heard the story of Lottie. He sobered when Jim told of the latest transaction at the green.

"Couldn't they have stopped them? They should have told the woman the truth about the puppy!" Sheila's voice was shrill, and she glared at both Jim and I in condemnation.

"No, they did the right thing. Not that I like it any more than you do Sheila, no good would have come from their interfering." Tenby stood up and walked to the door. He put his hand on the doorknob. "That Davies guy has nasty friends. You lot had better watch your backs!"

CHAPTER TWENTY TWO

Next morning I was awake at five thirty. I had prepared and laid out my clothes the previous night. Still in pyjamas, I looked down at them and shook my head. "No, those won't do." I placed them all back in the wardrobe. Five minutes later the bed was still not made, and clothes were strewn all over it.

A sudden thought had me rushing to the window and opening the curtains. Frost still lay in the ground, so it was cold. The sun was rising and promised a bright sunny day. I checked the weather app on my phone. It said clear and bright, but cold. That helped me make my decision. Smart black trousers, with my black ankle boots would look good with a plain white shirt and a grey fluffy chunky cardigan. Over it I had a new black-and-white checked jacket in warm tweedy mix. I thought that would be sombre and when I looked at it, it was so sombre it was funereal. Rummaging about in a drawer I found a bright red glittery scarf. I flung it over the top of the coat. That was it, a bright brilliant touch for the new me, and a simple outfit not to shock my mother. My clothes were now placed on the hanger, ready for my eleven o'clock appointment with my mother. My mother, how strange it was to say those actual words. The woman who brought me up, I'd always known was not my birth mother. I trusted her. Why had she lied to me? Why had she told me that my birth mother was dead?

Two faces sat at the bedroom doorway. Cleo's tail was swishing angrily, and Flora was trying to look starved. "It's far too early for your breakfast. But we are all up, so you might as well have it. I know you'll not give me any peace until you get it."

Both animals ate their breakfast as if they had been starved. As I watched them, a text sounded.

'I saw your lights on, you okay? Maggie.'

I replied at once, *'couldn't sleep, worried about meeting with mother. D'*

'no wonder. How about an early walk with Maisie and Flora?'

We walked along the path on the hillside above the burnt out cottages. On Maisie's arrival she had been so frightened of everything. Maisie was a beautiful brown and white Cavalier King Charles bitch, her puppies were different, they were both black and tan. It had taken ages before she ventured out of her box. Placed in the kitchen, it was no wonder that when she did come out, she clung to Maggie. So many hours had been spent with Maggie, that Maisie trusted her, and pined for her when she was absent.

Ben and Rosie had appeared with toys for all the puppies. Maisie had ignored all the lovely fluffy ones but had fallen in love with a horrible yellow rubbery chicken. It had been Ben's choice. Long dangling legs and yellow body were topped by a head with a cockerel type red crest. When Maisie walked with it in her mouth, the legs dangled one way and the red crest the other, almost tripping her up. Why she had fallen in love with such a horrible toy not one of us could understand.

"I thought a walk together with Flora might be good for Maisie. It will be her first proper walk, although I have taken her around the kitchen garden and the lawns. I thought this would be her first long outing, and as she knows and likes you and Flora it would be easier for her. But she's insisted on bringing that dreadful chicken thing!"

Maisie trotted along, with constant looks at Maggie and nervous little spurts. Flora bounced along smelling everything. She dashed to the very end of her extendable, and then ran back towards us. After a while, Maisie lost her nervousness and she too joined in with Flora. But still the chicken was firmly clamped in her jaws.

"Yesterday, the last of Maisie's pups were spoken for. Ben's friend insisted his parents come up and have a look at Lottie, the dachshund. Both parents were set against having a dog, but they fell in love with Maisie's last black and tan pup."

"What about Maisie? That's both her pups going now, what will happen to her?" I asked Maggie.

"You know quite well what's going to happen to Maisie! I couldn't inflict another upheaval on her. She's taken to me and honestly, I couldn't part with her." Maggie smiled down at the dog, happily trotting along beside us. "She's a sweetie, and she's so happy now. So different to that quivering wreck of a dog that was brought home. Do you think she remembers being here? It's not far from where she was found."

We were on the path along the top of the hill. The burnt cottages looked forlorn in their dereliction. Further along the valley had been where Alice had met her death. I shivered. It had been so dreadful, but at least some good had come out of it, I thought as I looked at Maisie. The morning was cold and there was still frost in patches on the ground. Our breath came out in tiny clouds and even the dog's breath hung in the air beside them. The cold did not deter them, they didn't seem to feel it and bounced along happily.

"It's such a peaceful spot this morning," said Maggie.

As she spoke, I felt a stinging in my arm. Maggie gave a shriek. Her hand flew up to her cheek. Blood was oozing from a wound.

"Down! Lie flat Maggie. Someone is shooting at us." We threw ourselves down, flat on the frosty path. Both dogs began licking our faces. They thought this was great fun. The shooting had stopped. I grabbed a stick lying beside the path, took off my hat, put it on the stick and held it high up in the air. Shots were fired at it. My new bobble hat had air vents! Maggie grinned at me.

"What are you laughing at?" I demanded.

"You! It's just like the movies," she snorted with laughter, despite the fear in her face. "It's some sort of pellet gun Daisy. Don't think it will kill us, but it can do some damage."

Putting my hand in my jacket pocket for my phone, a text came through.

'Crashed into a ditch, brakes failed. Jim'

I showed it to Maggie and began texting back.

'Gunman shooting at us on path.'

Another text came in from Martin. Obviously Jim had rung him and they had agreed that Martin would go to pick up Jim. Gerald was going to come and help us.

"It'll take Gerald quite a while to catch up to us. What the heck can he do when he gets here?" I muttered.

"I'm scared and furious and I'm getting very cold. How are we going to get back to the Priory, with that chap shooting at us. Neither dogs are properly trained, and they just keep running round us and licking us," wailed Maggie.

"He's obviously below us. I think we ought to move. Try to get back to the Priory. If we crawl further away from the edge, still keeping low, we should be out of his line of fire." As I spoke I began crawling, with an excited Flora loving this new game.

"I wonder how Jim is. Do think he was badly hurt?"

"He must be all right if he managed to text, and sort everything out. We need to make sure we don't get hurt." I glanced at Maggie's cheek, where the blood still dribbled down. "Or hurt anymore," I said through gritted teeth. "And these were new denim jeans. I'll never get the muck and grass stains out."

We had reached the furthest point from the edge and were up against a wall. Flora had decided she liked the stick that I'd used to poke up the hat and carried it along in her mouth. I took it from her to try my hat-trick again. I tried to, but she thought I wanted to play tug-of-war. Maggie started to giggle. Oh no, I thought, calm capable Maggie is verging on hysteria.

"Good girl Flora, can I borrow your stick for a moment? Just for a moment and I'll give it back." Flora sat back on her haunches and considered. Then she dropped the stick for me. I tried the hat-trick again. Nothing. We crawled along a bit further.

Another shot whistled past us. This time it was closer.

"He's climbing up the hill, if we don't hurry he'll be on top of us," Maggie whispered.

"Can you make it to the boulders, and bushes. Perhaps if we crawl down behind them, he may go past us," I hissed.

CHAPTER TWENTY THREE

The pile of bushes and boulders did not hide us from his immediate view. We heard him approach towards us. Then, he stood his gun raised at the ready. Tall, thin but not Ferret Face. A hoodie was pulled forward so little could be seen of his face, but it was enough to note the difference. The early morning sun had risen behind us and caught his eyes. A malicious glint flashed as he finally stood before us.

"Nosy old bags! Keep to yourselves and keep out of our business."

"You can't shoot us! Not at point-blank range," shouted Maggie.

"No, but I can shoot your dogs." He lowered his gun and levelled it at Flora and Maisie who now sat side-by-side.

"Oh no you don't!" I bent down, lifted up a rock and threw it at him. Laughing at me, he dodged to one side.

Flora suddenly gave a yip. She thought he was a friend. Every man to our Flora was a friend. Maisie dropped the rubber chicken and gave a tiny bark. I grabbed the chicken and squeezing it hard, flung it at the man. It was a type of dog toy with a shrill squealing noise when pressed tightly. The toy hit the man in the face, the noise of it unbelievable in the early morning silence. He screamed and squeaked. A silly girly scream for such a big man. Both dogs, thinking this was a great game, ran towards him. They jumped up at him. The gun dropped onto the grass as he flailed his arms wildly trying to hold his balance. Already off-balance with the chicken attack, the dogs sudden impetus towards him pushed him backwards over the edge. Both Maggie and I struggled to keep the dogs following him down the slope. Reeling their extendable leads in, we walked to the edge and stared over at the man.

"I don't think he's hurt, shame. If only it had been that cliff face that they threw Alice off... Threatening our dogs. I've a good mind to give him a taste of his own medicine." Maggie shouted at him and reached for the gun.

"No Maggie. Let's get home, we have to find out what happened to Jim. Go on ahead of me, my ankle hurts again. I'll only slow you down."

Gerald could be seen running towards us. Maggie reached him and gestured back towards me. I had both dogs, and they were becoming quite a handful. Thankfully, I passed him Lottie. Flora and I, with the gun limped home.

"Why have you got a gun Daisy?" Sheila's voice could be heard as she walked out of the Priory kitchen into the courtyard. There was envy in her question. Exhausted, and with intense pain now in the ankle, I could only wave at her and enter my cottage. A shower was my first priority, and then I promised myself that I could collapse. I could hear Sheila's exclamations and Maggie's replies as she told the story. I stood in the shower, the hot water easing some of the aches. I knew I'd be in agony tomorrow. But it could have been so much worse. If Sheila had been with us... And he could have shot the dogs.

Fully dressed, dirty clothes in the washing machine, I put the kettle on. I stood waiting for it to boil and thought about Jim. In the text he'd sent me, he said that he was unhurt. I had put him and his accident out of my mind. After all, getting shot, even though it was only with pellets, took priority

"Daisy! Daisy!" The doorbell rang.

"The door is open. Come in," I shouted. I knew I'd be having company, to save getting up, my door was unlocked and the coffeepot was already brewing.

Sheila barrelled in, excited as ever. "Are you all right? How's the ankle? Oh my, it's so swollen again. I have seen to Maggie's face, have you any gunshot wounds? Only a graze on your arm, and the ankle. Right, Daisy you go and sit down. I'll get a bag of frozen peas to put on it and sort out all the drinks."

"Jim? Anyone heard from Jim?" I managed to interrupt Sheila's flow of words.

"He is furious, the car is a write-off. Something or other underneath the car was badly smashed, and it's very important. It will cost a fortune to replace it."

"Never mind the car! What about him? Is he badly hurt?"

"Oh I don't know, all he could talk about was the car," Sheila said, frozen peas still in her hand. "Yes, all he could talk about was his wretched car, so he can't be badly hurt." She placed frozen peas on my ankle. "He's a man, he'd soon have told me if he was hurt."

"That's sexist, Sheila!" I protested.

"I'm over eighty five years of age. I'll say what I want," she said.

My visit to the care home had been cancelled. The clothes that I had chosen so carefully that morning, still hung in my wardrobe. I'd looked at them as I got out fresh clothes in exchange for my mucky ones. I didn't know whether I was pleased the visit was cancelled or whether I was sorry. Putting off the visit seemed to be a mixed blessing. It was arranged that I would go tomorrow morning.

The evening meal in the Priory kitchen that night had been subdued. Except for the dogs. Maisie was in her basket as usual, but with the one remaining puppy. It was leaving tomorrow. A young family in the next village were thrilled to get the pretty black and tan Cavalier pup. Franz and Hans had gone that afternoon. Sheila had been left with Lottie who had joined the others in the kitchen. She had greeted with great excitement Flora's arrival.

To my great astonishment Cleo had meowed outside the kitchen door. Jim had opened the door also surprised at her entrance. My cat stalked into the kitchen, glanced round at each dog and the puppy, then jumped onto a kitchen stool. A glance in my direction, a complete wash, and she settled down. Her vantage point on the kitchen stool gave her an overall view to watch the proceedings in the kitchen.

"She's frightened she's going to miss out on anything. Cats are such nosy creatures," laughed Sheila.

Cleo glared at Sheila. She was affronted by such remarks.

"Shall we discuss the day's happenings and…" Sheila began speaking.

Groans from all of us greeted this remark.

"Sheila, we are all exhausted after today's events. Please can we leave the in-depth discussion until tomorrow morning," pleaded Jim. The day's events had taken its toll on every one of us. I could see the lines on Jim's face had deepened throughout the day. The damage to his car had been devastating to him. He loved that car. Thankfully he had been unhurt but he was getting very fed up with ending up in an airbag again, after yet another incident!

Sheila's face fell, and she looked from one to the other hoping for some encouragement. Every head shook, exhaustion had overcome each one of us. All we could think of was our beds. Ageing bodies do not recover as quickly as we would have liked. Except for Sheila of course!

"How about a power breakfast again, with an in-depth discussion. Perhaps you could have an agenda all written out for us, Sheila," I said.

"Great! I'll get that done tonight, ready for

the morning." Sheila's face lit up with delight.

We all rose to go to our homes. Flora and Cleo joined me at the door, Lottie joined them.

"No you don't Lottie, you go with Sheila." I picked her up and handed the squirming dog to Sheila. Her indignant yips and whines could be heard as Sheila went down the hall corridor. My two pets sat and watched her go. Then they stared up at me. "No, you two are quite enough. I'm not taking on another pet." As I turned, I saw both Maggie and Martin watching me with strange smirks upon their faces. "What?" I questioned them.

"Nothing Daisy. Nothing at all, have a good rest and keep off the ankle." Maggie said, and Martin nodded agreement.

My bed never looked so inviting. The animals had refused to sleep in the lounge. I had been adamant, well, up to a point. Neither of them was ever going to set a paw on my bed! And this I meant. The basket was placed opposite my bed and I was firm about it. It was agreed between us all. Somehow, they knew I would not relent on this. I lay back upon my pillows, tuned in my audiobook, sipped my tea, and nibbled on my chocolate chip cookie. Bliss! Even my ankle had stopped throbbing. My phone rang. I looked at the display. Unknown caller. "Yes," I said warily.

"Hello Daisy. It's Nigel here."

CHAPTER TWENTY FOUR

I switched my phone off and placed it with extreme care on the bedside table. I wanted to fling it at the wall, but it was my new expensive one. I wanted to pace up and down the room in fury, but I couldn't because of my painful ankle. Damn the man! How did he get my new mobile number? Elsie I suppose, drat her. I reached for my phone and blocked Elsie's number, and that last unknown number. And switched my phone off. Wasn't technology wonderful? After that, I slept well. I woke refreshed, until all my aches and pains flooded in. It was at least thirty minutes after the pets breakfast time. But they had obviously sat in their basket watching and waiting for me to wake up.

"You are the best! Thanks for letting me sleep, you are absolute poppets." My landline rang, "Daisy I've tried to text you, but I couldn't get through, are you okay?" Maggie's concern was obvious in her voice.

"Sorry Maggie. I switched it off last night. Nigel rang, somehow he got my number, so I blocked his number, and switched off the phone."

"What did he want?" Maggie asked me.

"I don't know, and I don't want to know. I just cut him off and blocked his number and also Elsie's. I reckon she gave him my number."

"Martin and I will be with you in a few

minutes. We will walk Flora and Maisie, so you can rest your ankle."

"Great, I've just fed Flora. I'll put her harness on and have her ready for you."

With Flora out walking and Cleo pottering in the garden, I showered and dressed in peace and quiet. My ankle was better, not quite as swollen. I dressed with great care. Yesterday's visit to my newly discovered mother's care home had obviously been cancelled. Fortunately, she had not been told about our coming, so it hadn't mattered. Maybe we'd manage it today.

Sheila arrived at breakfast in the Priory kitchen, with a folder, clipboard, and laptop. At the sight of all this paraphernalia, Jim sent me a reproachful look. I shrugged my shoulders and grinned at him. Painkillers were very much in evidence at the breakfast table that morning, and most of us took great care in sitting down.

"Well? I've waited until we've eaten. Let the meeting begin." The clip board was flourished and Sheila settled back in her chair. Jim brought out his notebook and took the top off his fountain pen. "Jim, what actually happened? What are you going to do about it?" Sheila asked, pen raised to take notes.

"I was coming up to a narrow bend down by that old farmhouse. Do you know the one I mean?" At our nods, he continued. "I had previously met the local boy racers at that point, so I always slow down, and take the zigzag part of the bend carefully. Just as well, the brakes went spongy, and then nothing. Slow as I was going, it was still a hell of jolt into the hedge. The car took a lot of damage from the stone wall. I was fine, just back into the airbag again!"

"That was a definite attempt upon your life Jim. Any idea of when the car was tampered with?" Sheila asked him.

"That's what the police asked me. I leave it out in the courtyard overnight. Otherwise, I only park in crowded places like Stonebridge, or the community shop."

Martin spoke. "Last night, I ordered CCTV cameras and alarms for the courtyard and around the building. We obviously need extra security." There were nods of approval at this.

"Good," Sheila made an official note of this on her clipboard. "Now Martin and Gerald please, your reports."

Gerald had joined us for coffee, now a regular habit with him. Only while he worked on the puppy farm project, he had said. Somehow, I thought it would become a permanent habit, continuing long after the puppy farm project was over.

"Gerald came to help me to sort out the delivery. It had just been dumped any old how in the stable. We decided to separate the puppy from the dog food in different piles. Then we got a phone call from Jim about his accident and telling us that Daisy was being shot at. I went off with the car to pick up Jim, and Gerald rushed off down the path to help Maggie and Daisy." Martin said.

"Now Maggie and Daisy, tell us your story," Jim said.

"We went for a short walk along the top of the valley. It was ideal for Maisie to come out with us and Flora for the first time. We were near the large rock where Maisie and the pups had been found, and I felt a sting in my arm. Maggie had been shot in the face, and I could see blood trickling down her cheek. We fell flat on the ground and began to crawl back along the path towards home." I said.

"Daisy and Flora thought it a great game," Maggie continued with the story. "It was so difficult because we couldn't be certain if the shooter was still there. So Daisy borrowed Flora's stick and put her bobble hat on it. It's full of holes now. When he came towards us. Daisy threw that horrible rubber chicken at him, you know the one that Maisie loves. She brought it with her, and Daisy pressed it hard and it squeaked in the man's face. He gave such a silly scream, and the dogs rushed and jumped up at him. He tumbled backwards but not before I grabbed the gun that he had dropped."

Jim's face said it all! A despairing look crossed it but was quickly wiped off when I produced the hat. The holes were obvious. Our stories had all been told, our mugs refilled and the silence filled the kitchen. "It was well-planned, and well executed. What are they hoping to achieve? Are they trying to warn us off? Or are they trying to kill us as they did poor Alice?" Jim said.

I stood up whilst they were still discussing it. They seemed to be no nearer either a conclusion or a plan of action. But it was time for me to get ready and go. The others knew where I was going, all of them felt uncomfortable, and did not know what to say. What could they say? We all knew that this day for me would be life changing. I was going to meet Demelza, my twin sister Violet, and my birth mother in her nursing home.

I arrived early as usual and had to sit in the nursing home car park for twenty minutes. It was a pleasant car park. Trees and floral bushes promised a cheerful summer display. Not now, it was dark and dismal, and I felt a deep sense of foreboding creep over me as I sat trying to calm my nerves. How strange, this fit of the dismals was actually calming my nerves. Had I stumbled upon some new cure for nerves? I took a deep breath and stilled my twisting hands. A text came in, *'Good luck. Thinking of you, J.'* I texted back, *'thanks.'* The text had helped me, and I smiled at the kind thought. My bag over my shoulder, the car locked and I walked up the steps of the home to meet my family. As I walked from the car park I saw a few figures strolling about the grounds. They were warmly wrapped up, with carers alongside them. They seemed to be enjoying the fresh air and sunshine.

The stone steps led up to an open oak door. I entered into a bright open area and gave my name. The cheerful receptionist took me along a corridor to a small room.

"Please wait here. When Miss Trethowan comes I'll tell her you're here, and she can take you to meet Mrs. Trethowan." The receptionist left the room, leaving the door ajar behind her. It was a pleasant room, obviously a small interview room, or something similar. I sat on the edge of a chair, waiting for the others to arrive. The whole ambience and the decor of the home had surprised me. It was more like a hotel, a modern hotel, but with a cheerful intimate atmosphere. Footsteps could be heard along the corridor. I knew that noise. Only one pair of feet made that slurping sound. It was Demelza and her white wellington boots! My chair was just inside the door, and I could hear their voices clearly as they walked along the corridor. The footsteps ceased, obviously Violet wished to speak to Demelza before meeting me.

CHAPTER TWENTY FIVE

"I don't like it Demelza. Why now? Why has she never contacted us before? When she moved here I'm certain she discovered there was money, and an inheritance to grab. She never contacted us before, never!"

"But Violet, she never knew before. It was only when she was moving here that she discovered in the back of the picture..." Demelza began speaking.

"So she says! I reckon she's heard about that will. She's heard about the inheritance. It was Grandma's stupid idea that not only was Daisy alive, but she would return here to her family one day. Pathetic dreams of an old lady!" The contemptuous tone was evident even through the gap in the door.

"Violet! Your Gran had the sight. She knew this day would come and had prepared for it. Our solicitors will check out all Daisy's papers. There will be no doubt by the time they go through everything. They will make certain that Daisy is genuine."

"They better! I want no fortune hunter muscling in on our family inheritance." Her blunt reply and acid tones shocked me.

"I've known Daisy for admittedly only a short time, but she is truly the genuine article. To be honest Violet, she is as stunned by this as you are. She was going to leave it all alone, and never even contact you or your Mum. But both Jim and I said she'd got so far, she ought to contact you."

"Oh Demelza, so I've got you to thank for this fiasco. Thanks very much Demelza. Thanks very much indeed!"

Footsteps clattered loudly on the corridor and the door was abruptly pushed open. Violet, my twin sister entered the room followed by Demelza. I was introduced to my sister. She gave me a polite nod and a limp handshake.

We then walked along the corridor to my Mother's room. Violet my twin, resembled me, or rather as I had looked before my image change. She even wore a similar blouse and cardigan to those I had bought for myself some time ago. A desultory conversation grew between us. The not so subtle enquiries into my financial estate infuriated me. I could have set her mind at rest in an instant. But I didn't. Why not? I don't know, perhaps it was because I felt so hurt by her attitude. My adoptive father had inherited a business which he ran with a partner until his death. It was still a lucrative business and I was a sleeping partner, attending the required number of board meetings, and keeping abreast of its financial progress. That was another thing Nigel hated. He had always wanted me to sell out and take the money. But I couldn't, my adopted father had left the business and my inheritance tied up. There was no way I could liquidise the assets. My father had obviously distrusted Nigel. Now I was extremely grateful for his foresight. The chilly reception from Violet was echoed by my mother's peculiar attitude towards me. She stated categorically that I was an impostor. I was not her daughter. Demelza said I should continue to visit her as we left the room. Her doctor and nurse both said the same. I couldn't return. This had been a mistake and I couldn't take any more. Acceptance as a daughter, then a decision never to see me again was a possibility I had thought of. But this refusal to accept the birth certificate and the photo evidence was unexpected. Added to Violet's rejection, it decided me. I'd come and seen my birthmother and my twin sister, but it was best for all of us if I never saw them again.

On my way home I stopped in a layby. I didn't cry. I just sat and stared out across the panoramic views of Bodmin Moor. My phone gave the tone I always reserved for Jake.

"Mum, don't speak, just listen. We are coming home. Lisa is okay but she got bitten by a snake. She was bad for a couple of days. We finally realised that we are soft poms, and the Australian outback is too much for us. We are coming to join you in Cornwall. Possibly set up a business, don't know what, but will sort it out when we get home. Can you find a place for us to rent? Anything reasonable will be a palace after the outback. Love you Mum." The phone went dead. I hadn't said a word, I don't think I knew what to say. After the cruel disappointment of my visit to the care home, I felt overjoyed at Jakes news.

At the evening meal I related what had happened at the care home.

"Are you all right Daisy?" Sheila's hand grabbed mine, and she leant her face close to mine searching for signs of distress.

"Actually I am all right," I squeezed her arthritic hand with care. "Honestly, I'm surprised at myself, I really am okay. You all know that I didn't have high hopes. Violet thinks I'm after the inheritance, and my mother refuses to believe that I'm her daughter. I discovered my true roots are here in Cornwall, and even close to the Priory. It's fate that brought me here. I belong to this area, and that's enough for me."

"Thank goodness," sighed Maggie. "We've been so anxious and fearful of what would happen, and what you would find out. It's wonderful that you found out that you belong here, and you've come home."

I got sympathetic looks from them all, which made me very embarrassed. Then I jumped up in my chair, "I've got good news," I declared smiling at them. "Lisa, my soon-to-be daughter-in-law, was bitten by a snake."

"That doesn't sound like good news!" Jim exclaimed.

"Oh dear. Is she all right? Has she recovered from it?" Sheila asked me.

"Yes, she's fine. Lisa disliked the outback and was miserable when they were searching for gold. She was staying for Jakes sake. But the long journey back to get treatment for the snakebite, decided for both of them. They want to come back to the UK, and they want to come back to Cornwall to live near here." I sat back in my chair and beamed at them. My disappointment over the mother/sister debacle faded into insignificance at Jakes news.

"What will they do?" Jim asked, ever the practical one.

"They don't know yet. They're hoping to rent somewhere and perhaps set up their own business. They've been gold mining out in Australia, I suppose they like being their own boss."

Sudden exclamations from around the table alerted me to what I just said. "Oh, goldmining... What a strange coincidence."

"That's not what Demelza will say," said Maggie. There was general laughter around the table. "She will say that it's an omen, that it was meant to be."

After the meal by mutual consent we adjourned to the library to discuss the day's events and to plan our next move. We have got to take down that devil Davies, Martin had said to general approval. Yesterday's events had shown how desperate our enemy had become. I had however been completely drained of all my energy. The day's emotional events had tired me. After a few moments, I made my apologies and left. Entering my cottage I was greeted by Cleo and Flora. I let them out and stood on the doorstep. The dark mass of the moor stretched away into a deepening night sky, and my breath came out in tiny clouds as the cold of the approaching frost struck my face. Neither animal lingered, business attended to, they dashed in sitting hopefully beside their bowls. Night-time treats dispensed, and then it was a mad dash for the sofa to pick the comfiest spot.

I stood at the kitchen sink, staring out into the darkness. Then it came. The storm of tears built up throughout the day broke. I'd laughed and talked about possible rejection, I'd even expected it. When it actually happened, I found I could not pass it off as lightly as I'd hoped. The wonderful news from Jake had kept me buoyed up during the day and evening. Now I sat on the sofa, my pets cuddling close to me, and sobbed my heart out.

CHAPTER TWENTY SIX

An hour later, I wiped my eyes with my now sodden tissue, and went into the kitchen. The whisky bottle, and half bottle of white wine always kept in the fridge for Sheila were so tempting. I opened the fridge, got out the milk and put on the kettle. My resolution failed me when I saw that Maggie had left her fruit cake tin behind. Perhaps it was empty? I hoped it was empty. But no, there was another large slice left, obviously for me. Well, I couldn't let that go to waste, could I?

A text came in as I returned to the sofa with mug, buttered fruitcake, and of course a cat and dog treat.

Are you okay? I saw your lights on, J.

I replied, *I'm fine thanks. I did have a crying jag, but fine now. Maggie's fruitcake helps!*

If you need to chat, just text, J

Thanks, appreciate that. I texted him back and I meant every word of that text. Any one of the group in the Priory would come in an instant if I called them. Never, when married to Nigel, had I felt this wonderful support and care. That thought brought me to the realisation that Nigel had to be removed completely from my life. Tomorrow I would compose a polite email stating in no uncertain terms my feelings.

Next morning, my eyes were still red rimmed but I felt better. The nervous anticipation was over. I'd finally found out about my family. On entering the Priory kitchen I was surprised to see Gerald. Then I realised he was sitting now in what had become his place, so I shouldn't have really been surprised at all.

"Hello Daisy. We decided last night right after you gone to bed, Jim, and Martin and I are going reconnoitring." His smile was broad, as he beamed at me. "Yes, we will climb down from the moor, coming back along the Valley Ridge towards the Priory. We'll pass Hilltop farm and Alice's cottage."

"We're going to be coming at it from a different angle. We might spot something we've never noticed before," said Jim as he entered the kitchen and sat down.

Maggie stood, her hands on hips and shook her head at them. "And what they are avoiding telling you, is that you will drop them off at their starting point."

Martin had now taken his place at the table, and the three men looked hopefully and slightly shamefacedly at me. It was a peculiar mixture to have on a face, but all three men managed that identical expression.

"Of course I'll take them. I've a couple of paintings to drop into the gift shop. It won't be much out of my way," I answered.

"Are they selling your paintings now?" Maggie asked.

"One has sold unframed, but these two I want framed. The mounts and frames need to be chosen to suit them. If they look good, paintings sell for more money. Jeff has a good eye and does a superb job."

"Jeff?" Jim asked, a strange look crossing his face.

"Oh Jeff! Watch out for him Daisy. He's older than you, but still reckoned to be a heartbreaker," warned Maggie.

"Yes Maggie, I've realised that already."

"Has he asked you out for a date? They say if he fancies you he's not slow in asking for a date." Sheila's eyes sparkled with interest.

"Of course he has! Every time I go in. But I think he's beginning to realise that he's wasting his time," was my reply.

A satisfied look passed over Jim's face, it was only fleeting, but I caught it.

"There is going to be a delivery coming for me," declared Sheila. Her excited face told us it was going to be something special.

"Come on, what are you getting delivered?" Maggie asked her.

"Guess? All of you guess?"

"As long as it's not another puppy," was a grumpy reply from Jim.

"A new outfit," was Gerald's reply. Obviously he was still out of touch with Sheila and her interests.

"A new iPad or iPhone," said Martin as Sheila looked inquiringly at him.

"Better, but still far off the mark. Daisy what's your guess?"

That overeager grin, coiled tension in her slight frame meant that it was something big, and possibly outrageous.

"A Harley Davison?" I answered her.

"Nearly! Daisy is the warmest," she clapped her hands and grinned delightedly.

I don't know who wore the most appalled expression on their face. It was a close contest, but not one of us knew what to say in reply to that remark from Sheila.

"Okay Sheila, I may be the nearest, but what have you got coming?" I asked.

"It's a special mobility scooter with five wheels! It can go over rough terrain. I want to go with Ben and Rosie on their walks. My knees are playing up and I find it difficult to go far with them. This way I can go further and over rough ground!"

Cries of encouragement and support were more than usually enthusiastic. That image that had burst into all of our minds, of Sheila hurtling around Cornish lanes, with poor eyesight and dodgy knees in leather on a Harley had been horrifying for all of us. A mobility scooter seemed a better option. But it was Sheila I remembered, nothing could be discounted when she was around!

The men were duly dropped off at the designated point. Gerald and Martin were loaded up with bulging rucksacks and odd shaped lumpy things hanging off them. Jim had a slick, well-worn leather satchel bag slung over his shoulder. It didn't bulge or seem overstuffed. I would have loved to see what was in it. No doubt it was crammed with the smallest most up-to-date techie stuff imaginable.

Stonebridge was quiet. The tourists had not arrived, a cold wind and the forecast of snow had kept people at home. The gift shop was small but on the main street. It was warm when I entered it. Jeff worked at his picture framing in the back, and during this quiet period came through to serve any customer. Locals did not require gifts or mementos, his only trade was from artists for framing, and for the unusual birthday cards he displayed. The usual flirting banter over with, we got down to the serious business of mounts and frames. The right colour mount with the right colour and width of frame made the most of any painting. It had all been settled satisfactorily between us, when I became conscious of a figure looming outside the shop window.

I opened the door and Jeff called out to my retreating back. "See you soon Daisy, you always brighten my morning!" I turned laughed at him, and waved goodbye. Closing the door I turned to be confronted by Nigel.

CHAPTER TWENTY SEVEN

"Who was that?" Was Nigel's first question as he glared through the glass door at Jeff.

"Excuse me," I said coolly. It had taken a moment to get over my initial shock at having my ex-husband standing before me. He looked smaller somehow, and shabbier. That confident manner he always wore seemed to have vanished.

He began to speak. "Shall we go for a coffee? At that hotel over there? That's where I'm staying. The coffee isn't too bad. Oh! Of course you have to have your everlasting tea stuff!"

Why did that remark ignite such a fury within me? Why after all the insults, the repeated lies, and the dalliance with other women, had nothing infuriated me more? That remark about my preference for tea, as if it was a crime, an aberration, or a strange peculiarity enraged me. My new friends automatically made me a cup of tea, expected me to have tea. But Nigel still sneered at it after all these years. We were blocking the pavement. Even I, mad as I was, did not fancy a row on Stonebridge High Street.

"Okay, we'll go to the hotel."

The lounge was gloomy, it was obviously not a coffee hotspot. The lunchtime trade had not started, and we were on our own in the cavernous room. I could hear the constant roar of traffic outside. The quiet of the hotel was broken only by distant voices, obviously coming from the kitchen preparing the lunchtime meals. We found a table near to the window. Crimson velvet curtains added to the sombre atmosphere, and the swirly patterned carpet beneath our feet deadened all sound. Silence grew around us, and I didn't know what to say.

"This is pleasant Daisy. I wanted to catch up with you. See how you're getting on. Couldn't quite understand you coming down here." A waitress arrived with his coffee and a small teapot, hot water, and cup and saucer for me. I smiled my thanks for the nice presentation of my tea. I began pouring it out immediately, I didn't like it stewed. I found concentrating on my tea put off the moment when I had to look at my ex-husband. I was going tell him exactly what I thought of him. Regardless of any atmosphere coming from my side of the table, Nigel kept on talking. "Elsie has found you a lovely bungalow near to her. I'll meet you there and advise you on whether it's a good buy or not. It's bigger than the last one she sent you, room for more than one person there!" He gave me his trademark roguish smile.

It didn't work. The realisation struck me that it hadn't worked on me for many years. Why had I stayed so long with this boring man? I'd drink all my tea and tell him word for word that email I had composed to him last night. I remembered it, every word. And would find it easy to tell him, face-to-face. After his coffee he smiled, what he assumed was another winning smile, and placed his hand on mine.

I withdrew my hand. My teacup was empty, I placed it on the saucer, stood up and slung my bag over my shoulder. "I do not want to see you again. There will be no future contact between us. I have signed a 99 year lease upon my cottage. My life is now here, and you and Elsie have no part in it. I told Elsie not to give you my phone number or my address. In future, any contact from Elsie or you will be considered harassment and I shall take legal advice. Goodbye Nigel."

My walk out of the hotel was calm and unhurried. That look on his face was priceless. Whatever he expected from me it had not been that. Standing outside the hotel I took in a deep cold breath. I felt good. I was free from my past. The future was going to be mine. At my age I realised that it may be very short, but it would be lived to the full on my terms. On that I was determined.

I drove into the courtyard to be confronted by a crowd. As I parked, the figures resolved themselves into Maggie, Sheila, Sheila's daughter Lesley with her children Ben and Rosie, Demelza and two strange men. Lesley's car was parked behind a strange van. They were all clustered round a jubilant Sheila who sat upon a mobility scooter that looked like a small tractor.

Maggie strode over to me as I got out of my

van. "She's beside herself, threatening to travel all over Bodmin Moor on it." We both laughed and then she took a good hard look at me. "What's happened Daisy? I can tell something has happened. You look different, sort of smug."

I grinned at her. "Tell you all about it later, let's sort out Sheila." Thoughts of Nigel faded from my mind as I went forward to inspect the new mobility scooter. "So this is the new Sheilamobile?"

"Isn't it great?" Sheila grabbed my arm. "Tomorrow we'll go along the bridle path Daisy. You'll come with me? Won't you?" Her claw like hand gave my arm urgent tweaks. I knew what she meant. That bridleway led along the valley towards Hilltop farm, the farm belonging to Davies. But it was a public path and used often by locals and horse riders.

"Of course, I can't wait to escort our new motorised Sheila," I smiled down at her.

Maggie put her hand on Sheila's shoulder, her other hand on mine. "Now you two, you have got to keep out of trouble!"

"We are not the ones who arrived back with yet more puppies!" Sheila shot back at Maggie.

Laughter greeted that and then Ben added his voice. "Daisy do bring more puppies back! We'd love more puppies!"

"No more puppies," was shouted in unison by everyone in the courtyard, except the two delivery men and the children.

The hairs began to rise at the back of my neck. Someone was watching me, I could sense it. Nigel stood by his car at the entrance archway. He stood staring at me. His glance encompassed the group surrounding me. Ben's cheerful face laughing up at me, Sheila's hand on my arm and Maggie standing beside me, one hand on my shoulder. Nigel stood and looked at me. He could see it all in one glance. I was laughing as I had never done with him. Surrounded by friends and happy in my new life, I had embarked on a journey alone in Cornwall that now provided me with everything I could have wished for. Nigel stared at me, then walked away to his car. He walked out of my life again. This time it meant nothing to me. Nigel no longer meant anything to me, no longer could he hurt me. I hoped he realised that.

"Daisy, we'll go in the morning, okay?" Sheila said.

"Yes Sheila, that will be great, I'm looking forward to it." I replied.

At the evening meal three exhausted men sank into the chairs at the kitchen table. The day had been cold but sunny, and they each sported a red face from the wind and sun.

"Did you find anything?" Maggie asked them.

"Nothing conclusive. We took lots of photographs and took GPS details from each spot we photographed. We'll enlarge them and check for anything that points to an entry or hidden gateway. We should find something," enthused Martin.

"Difficult terrain but I'm hopeful that our enlargement exercise will bring something forward that we would normally miss," Jim agreed.

"Martin, I've been wondering, are you going to move into the other apartment that Arabella and Hugo lived in?" Maggie asked Martin. The apartment was large and spacious. It had been empty since Hugo the former owner had gone to America. Renovations to the bathroom and kitchen had been done, it only needed the main bedroom and lounge to be decorated and furnished properly.

Martin stroked his beard and looked down at his plate. He pushed a large piece of broccoli around and around until it disintegrated into a green mush. His fork stilled and he looked up at Maggie. "I thought about it. I've even been in and walked around it several times. I know that you'll all think that I am mad, but I find it too big. The cottage suits me, and I feel comfortable in it. I'd rattle around on my own in that huge apartment. So, no Maggie, I'm staying in my cottage."

"Well thought out Martin. I agree with you these cottages have everything we need. If you're happy in it why move? That apartment still needs renovations to finish it off, that will take some time. Stay where you are and enjoy the cottage," said Jim.

A text came into my phone. *Working very late, about 1am. Tenby.* I frowned as I read it.

"Trouble?" Sheila asked.

"No, it's just Tenby warning me that he'd be

late home," I replied.

"Why did he have to let you know?" Maggie asked.

"Because of Flora! Every time he gets out of his car and walks to his cottage she gives a couple of barks. She knows it's him, and she won't settle until he calls a good night to her. If I know he's going to be in late at that time I don't worry about her barking, I know it's not a burglar. It's a daft system, but it works because I know it's Tenby." This was met by a shaking of heads and amused smiles.

Sure enough, barking came from Flora at one thirty. But it wasn't the usual barks she gave for Tenby's arrival. These rose in volume and were accompanied by shouts, yells and Tenby's loud blaring car horn pressed again and again.

CHAPTER TWENTY EIGHT

I threw on my dressing gown and rushed to the window overlooking the courtyard. Tenby stood with one hand on his horn, and the other holding his phone and was speaking urgently into it. Jim was rushing out towards him, with a sleepy Martin following him. I noted that for once Jim was actually ready for bed. Clad in a navy blue dressing gown he still looked smart and ready for action. I opened the window and shouted to Tenby, knowing that if I opened the front door Flora would rush out to greet him. In all the noise and confusion, Flora was still barking, her voice shrill and anxious.

"What is it? What's happening?" I shouted through the window at the men. Both Tenby and Jim turned to look at me. Even in the dim light from my cottage front door, and Tenby's headlights, I saw their faces whiten with fear. "What is it? What's wrong?" This time my voice carried a definite note of anxiety.

"Stay there Daisy! Do not open your front door! Stay there." Tenby shouted, his voice now an almighty bellow of fear and urgency.

"But what's wrong? What is it?" I repeated, my voice now quavering with fright. I did not know what had alarmed both men. I didn't need to! Their white faces scared me enough. There was no need for explanations. I knew whatever it was, it was bad, very bad!

Jim was approaching my front door with slow careful steps. Tenby grabbed his arm and pulled him back. Both men were staring intently at something at the door. I stood on my tiptoes to peer over the window ledge to see what they were looking at.

"There's a bomb at your front door! Don't open it, the door may be the trigger." At Tenby's words I drew back slowly and carefully from the open window. "I've alerted the bomb squad. Do not open any doors, or even windows now until they have been checked. I found the chap in the courtyard when I drove in. When he saw me he ran across the fields. I reckon that I interrupted his work," explained Tenby.

I saw that Jim was on his phone, obviously contacting all the others in the Priory. Flora had now subsided into a heap, her barking fizzled out and she was staring up at me with a worried expression on her face.

"Come on, you and Cleo are going for an outing. Won't it be fun?" I found Flora's basket and put her in it, then plonked Cleo in beside her. Both animals settled down quietly, as if they understood it was an emergency.

The voices continued outside the window and I listened to them as I raced into my bedroom, throwing on jeans, a sweatshirt and grabbing my heaviest coat. My handbag was in the kitchen, and I flung in anything important as I was passing it.

"So we wait for the bomb squad," said Martin, wrapping his checked dressing gown tighter around his body as he began shivering. It was cold out in the courtyard, I gave Martin that. But I felt that his nerves had taken hold of him again.

Not unkindly Tenby pushed Martin towards his car. "Sit in there, it's still warm from my journey. Nothing you can do."

My phone rang. "What's wrong Daisy? What's going on? Maggie has joined me in my apartment. Do you know what's happened? Tenby has just texted orders to us."

"Yes, Sheila, when he came back late into the courtyard, he surprised an intruder. That's why he hooted his horn and shouted to everyone."

"He did that all right! I was asleep and thought I was on a ship and it was a foghorn. Took me ages to realise what it was," grumbled Sheila.

"I opened my window to see what was happening. When they turned to look at me they saw there was a bomb wired up to my front door." I could hear the gasps and muttered oaths that came from both women over my phone.

"This guy likes explosives, doesn't he? So they think he may have put others around the place?" Maggie asked me.

"They don't know, that's why the bomb squad is coming, and we have to stay put in doors and..." I never finished speaking.

A loud explosion shattered the night. Tenby's horn had long ceased its urgent summons, and the only noise had been the murmurs of the three men as they talked together in the courtyard. This noise echoed around the courtyard, the confined space making the sound ring in my ears. Then stars and sparkling flowers erupted into the air followed by golden streamers of sparks from behind the disused stable cottages. Tenby was on the phone again immediately. "Fire Brigade now!"

My phone rang again. "What's happened? Are you all right?" Maggie's voice was frightened now.

"It's a load of fireworks, rockets and loud bangers. Looks as if they are behind the disused stables."

Sirens grew closer and the courtyard became full of vehicles, shouts of men and over it all the erupting of fireworks gave an unearthly glow. The scene resembled a mediaeval picture of hell. Orange flames were against the sky, and behind the empty windows of the stable. Men were dashing about, only seen as dark silhouettes against the firework display. It was a frightening and confusing nightmare. All at once the flames died down. The firework display had finished but the hubbub still continued. Men moved about, but now in a purposeful controlled manner. That initial urgency had gone. The bomb squad guy came and looked at my front door, and then approached my open window. I had moved well back from doors and windows, but he saw me and called in to me.

"I'll check your back door. If that's okay I'll get you and your animals out. Get yourself, and them ready by the back door."

Handbag over my shoulder, warm coat buttoned up to my chin and a pet basket in my hand, I stood in my kitchen waiting.

The back door burst open and a large man in bomb squad gear helped me out, grabbing the basket from me. He led me round to the lane outside the Priory. Here Tenby's car been put to use as a temporary refuge for Priory residents and their pets alongside the SUV. Maisie and Maggie were already settled in the SUV when I joined them.

"There are no more devices. Only the one in the stables which had a timer and the one at your cottage door. They were small devices, meant to alarm with the firework bang, and then sparkly stars. They were only fireworks and meant to alarm us," said Jim who had walked up to the SUV after talking to the bomb squad guys. "Obviously a warning for us. If we don't mind our own business, he could get serious and they would be real bombs."

"Is it safe to go back into our homes?" Sheila asked. Her voice was no longer excited, it held the weariness of a tired old lady.

"Not long now, we'll just wait for everyone to leave before we return to our homes." Jim replied.

The fire brigade began to leave, the bomb squad guys were packing and Tenby stood in a huddle with his men. Into this chaos came a taxi. The driver poked his head out of the window and shouted out at the group. Anxious to make himself heard over the noise of the departing men, he opened the door and bellowed at us. "Is this Barton Croft Priory?"

Tenby shouted back. "Yes it's Barton Croft Priory. What the hell are you doing up here at this time of night?"

CHAPTER TWENTY NINE

The taxi driver shut his door and drove right into the courtyard. When the taxi came to a stop, a door was flung open and tall young man jumped out.

"Mum! Mum what's happening? Are you okay?"

"Jake? Jake is that really you? You're in Australia!"

He rushed up to me, giving me a hug after reassuring himself that I was in one piece. "What's going on here? What are all the emergency vehicles for?"

I extricated myself from his hug to see Lisa approach me. "Lisa! Are you all right after your snakebite? Why are you home? Why have you come back so quickly?" My jumbled questions tumbled out of my mouth. This mad night was becoming even stranger and more peculiar. Now my son was here. I gave myself a surreptitious pinch, I was awake. That pinch hurt me.

"Come on everyone, into the Priory kitchen. We all need to get warm and get some hot drinks into us." We turned to see Jim ushering everyone towards the Priory. The vehicles and men had almost gone, including the taxi.

"The taxi! I haven't paid," Jake exclaimed as his eyes followed the disappearing lights down the lane.

"Paid and tipped. You can owe me," Jim said, and thrust out his hand towards Jake.

"Welcome to the Priory. As you can see your Mum is taking her dislike of boredom to the extreme again!"

At my affronted glare at Jim, I saw Jake and Lisa both grin, and both hugged me. "I'll bet Elsie's tucked up in bed with her cocoa," laughed Jake.

"After tonight's drama I'm beginning to wonder if Elsie didn't have the right idea after all," I muttered.

"Hot drinks and food in the kitchen. Bring all the animals, they can have a run around with each other after being cooped up in their baskets," said Maggie.

"Will there be any chocolate chip cookies? Even in Australia our mouths watered at the very sound of them?" Jake asked.

Maggie grinned with pleasure, and patted him on the shoulder, "there's a fresh batch in the tin."

The chat in the Priory kitchen was about plane journeys, the long haul from Australia, fireworks made to look like bombs, and the rival merits of cookies as opposed to cupcakes. It took the edge of the nights drama and stress.

"How long are you staying for?" Sheila asked the question that had been hovering on the tip of my tongue.

I was desperate to know why they were here, unannounced and in the middle of the night. But in all the hubbub with everyone there, I hadn't got round to asking them. Immediately Jake and Lisa's face changed, startled I saw there were even tears in Lisa's eyes.

"What's wrong? What's happened?" I asked.

"My dad is in hospital. A drunk driver crashed into him, and he is still unconscious. We were planning to fly home. But when we heard the news we managed to get an earlier flight."

In the middle of the gasps of dismay, Sheila's voice cut through the chatter and straight to the point as usual. "Why have you come here then? Why come to the Priory?"

"My mum and dad live in the country, there are no buses, and my mum can't drive. Jake wondered..." Lisa couldn't continue speaking, she cast a pleading look towards me. Her hand twisted the long curl that hung over her shoulder. Its length was new to me. Obviously hairdressers were not very handy in the outback. I liked it, long hair suited her.

"Of course you can take the van. I filled her up yesterday so you don't have to worry about fuel for a while. When you want to leave? Do you want to stay the night and rest?" I asked.

"We had a good rest on the plane, and on the train down to Cornwall. Lisa would like to set off right away if you don't mind. As you know, her parents live near Bude, it's not that far. But what about insurance Mum?"

Jim had been messing about in his phone for a little while. "It will cost more because of the immediacy, but it's only a phone call and it's done. Here Daisy, I've got it all set up. Finish it off with your credit details, and Jake is good to go." I was delighted to get it done quickly, but still irritated at Jim's highhandedness. As usual!

As we stood by the van, I kissed them goodbye. Everybody wished Lisa's father well as Maggie rushed up towards us. "Here you are, salad, cold meats, cheese and rolls. There is fruitcake and more cookies. There's plenty in there because I expect your mum won't have thought about food." Jake and Lisa thanked Maggie profusely, got into the van and left for Bude. I watched them go, absolute delight at having them home again, and worry about the seriousness of the injuries that Lisa's father had sustained.

Jim and Martin had joined Tenby who had just arrived back in a huddle in the courtyard. "What's wrong now?" I asked.

"Nothing Daisy, we just want to sort out a rota to keep watch. Your cottage has the best view of anyone coming through the archway and kitchen garden gate. Do you mind if we sit inside your lounge window. Your window seat is ideal for a look out."

"No, of course not," I replied. But I did mind. All I wanted was peace and quiet. Too much had happened today, my brain was frazzled. Nigel, Jake and Lisa, my mother and sister were all dancing around in my head in a bizarre merry-go-round fashion. My arrival at the Priory had been as a single person, facing a solitary life in my old age, no husband, and no child nearby. That had been my future, or so I thought. I had resigned myself to a solitary life with my cat, my painting, and lots of healthy walks. I thought I had adjusted to it and perhaps I had. The arrivals into my life of Nigel my ex, and now Jake and Lisa, with my newfound birth family was bad enough. Fires, puppies galore, shooting attempts and firework bombs all added to the peculiar mix my poor brain was trying to process. And now I was going to have to cope with the stream of watchers or sentries or whatever they were going to call themselves all night long. "You all know where the kettle is. Sort out your rota, I will take an early morning one. Now I must get to bed!"

"You're exhausted Daisy, go to bed and have a good night's sleep. We'll wake you up for an early morning shift," said Jim.

Snuggling down in my bed, I realised that I did feel safer knowing someone was on guard in my lounge. But I wouldn't tell them that. Surely tonight would pass without any more incidents.

We were a weary lot that gathered around the breakfast table. All except Sheila, who was bubbling with excitement and enthusiasm. "We're going for our walk Daisy. You promised you'd come with me on my first outing."

Of course I had. But I had not realised how exhausted I would feel when the time came. But that look of joyful anticipation on Sheila's face could not be squashed. Swallowing hard I replied to her. "Of course Sheila, it should be great fun. Where will we go for our first journey?"

"What about the bridleway from the Priory alongside the river that runs along the valley bottom?"

"Sheila, I'm not going sleuthing with you on a mobility scooter."

"No, no it's just to see how good the scooter is on the bridleway. Ben and Rosie love the Riverwalk. No detecting Daisy," Sheila replied, but she wouldn't look me in the eye.

Maggie was standing at the kitchen sink. "Sorry Sheila, but it's beginning to rain. The forecast is good tomorrow, I'd postpone your trip till then. Daisy, as you're not going with Sheila this morning, I'd like you to come to Wisteria cottage with me. I have some leaflets and notices to hand into Violet for the WI."

"No way Maggie. I'm not going to that cottage again ever."

Jim was sitting at the table sunk into gloom. He'd been speaking to his garage and his precious car was a mess. It would be some time before all the parts could be delivered and fitted. The lines on his face had deepened over the past weeks, and the obvious stress and exhaustion was taking its toll.

"Don't be so melodramatic Daisy. You're going to be living in the same village with her. Surely you can be civilised enough to be on speaking terms with her. That's all that is required of both of you. Don't tell me that you're not curious to see inside the house where you were born, and where your family have lived for generations."

Jim was correct. I wasn't keen to see inside Wisteria cottage, I was desperate! He was also correct that living in the same village and taking part in the communal activities required a modicum of civility between us. The rain was now battering against the kitchen window, so no outing with Sheila was possible today. The ground would be too muddy for the mobility scooter, even if it stopped raining.

"Okay Maggie, I'll go and get ready. See you at eleven." I left Maggie and Jim. I had agreed to go with her, but I wasn't looking forward to meeting my twin sister again. I really didn't want to face her. What would I say? What would her reaction be towards me? On my last trip to Wisteria cottage, her attitude and that of her dog had been unpleasant, I really couldn't face that again. But I had promised Jim and Maggie, so I would get ready and meet Maggie at the SUV.

CHAPTER THIRTY

"Daisy, can I talk to you privately?" Gerald's voice was nervous. He stood on my doorstep blinking furiously through his thick glasses. I was surprised to see him, it was unusual for him to seek me out.

"Yes of course, come in. I was making tea for myself or would you prefer coffee? Sit down. On a chair would be best. There's no pet fur on it, the sofa is covered in fur." I made his coffee, got my tea, and brought the mugs in, setting them down on the coffee table. Gerald sitting on the sofa had a surprised but delighted smile on his face. Cleo and Flora had snuggled up on either side of him.

"Thank you Daisy. I think they like me."

"They seem to be happy beside you. They have accepted you as their friend." Sipping my tea I smiled at the man. Obviously unused to animals, they had in a few moments enslaved yet another fan.

"I've come to you Daisy first of all." Gerald took an overlarge gulp of his coffee, coughed a little, and then put his mug down on the table. "Sam is..." His voice tailed away.

"Sam is the gunman who sends me postcards, and who shot Jim?" I said over my mug.

"Sam is my older brother," Gerald blurted out. Whatever Gerald was going to say I had not expected that. All I could do was stare at him. My mug wobbled in my hand, and I placed it down carefully onto the coffee table. I took a deep breath, trying to keep my mouth closed on the outpouring of words that I wanted to shout out at him. I sat back in the chair and placed my hands carefully onto my lap. And I waited for his story.

"My parents divorced when I was five years old. Sam was two years older and went with my mother, whilst I stayed here with my father. My mother was what they called a wild child, my dad was a bookish schoolteacher. Although we grew up totally different people in different places, we are actually quite close. He despairs of my bookish pastimes, whilst I've been horrified at his lifestyle and choices." His hand went out for coffee, he took a slurp from the mug, and then glanced over the mug to gauge my reaction. Processing this news was difficult, but I realised that it did explain a lot that had puzzled me.

Keeping my face in a neutral expression I said, "and now you want to tell me, why?"

"Sam is unhappy abroad. He says he didn't realise how happy he'd been living here on Bodmin Moor. Whilst he stayed with me here he'd helped out an old friend of his, renovate old motorbikes. He loves tinkering with machines, especially motorbikes. His friend has offered him a partnership in a garage, on condition that he goes straight."

"I see," I said. Although I didn't, but felt he needed encouragement.

"Sam plays loud music, mostly rock 'n' roll. I like silence whilst I work on my maps and

Knights Templar research. Martin is going to renovate another one of the stables into a cottage. He's offered me one." Gerald put his coffee cup on the table with great care. It was needed because his hand was shaking. A pleading look crossed his face, and he stared intently at me. "I love being up here at the Priory with you all. I love working in the library. But if I move into this cottage, it will only be if you agree to it. Sam can move into the cottage where I'm staying at the moment. Actually the cottage belongs to both of us, we inherited it from our father. What do you say Daisy? Will you let Sam come back? And will you agree to me moving into a stable cottage here at the Priory? He has promised to go straight. You won't be in any danger from him, he promised me."

"Will he go straight? Are you certain that we won't be in any danger from him?" I asked Gerald, knowing that I was repeating his words. But I had to make it clear, there had to be no doubt.

"No, no Daisy. Sam is so grateful to you all, especially you Daisy, for accepting me into the group. He knows that I find it hard..." Again, his voice tailed away and I saw tears gather at the back of his eyes. "I love the Priory and you all, I don't make friends easily and all of you..." He gulped and drew a large handkerchief from his pocket and wiped his eyes. Both animals seemed to sense his emotions and understood that he was upset. Cleo licked his hand, and Flora stretched up to lick his ear. "Oh they like me too!" Gerald's eyes watered, and his face began to pucker.

"Biscuits! I forgot the biscuits." I got to my feet and rushed to the kitchen for the biscuit tin. I was no good at coping with emotional scenes, but one coming from Gerald was definitely out of my skill set. When I sat down with a plate of biscuits between us, Gerald had wiped his eyes and put the handkerchief away.

"You have to tell Jim about Sam," I warned him. "I don't think you need explain anything to the others. Tenby may get to hear of Sam's return and guess, but he has no evidence against him. I won't say anything, but I do warn you and Sam, if there is the slightest return to his old ways, I will get Martin to ask you to leave." Gerald's face broke into a broad smile, and then he looked worried at how Jim would accept this situation. So I texted Jim, made fresh coffee and put out more biscuits. On Jim's arrival, Gerald explained it all to him.

For a long moment Jim looked at Gerald. Then he turned to me, the expression on his face unreadable. "Daisy, what do you really feel about it? What do you feel about the return of Sam?"

I shrugged, "I would far rather the wretched man sat on a sunny beach as far away from us as possible. But if he goes straight and causes us no bother, we'll give it a go. At least he will stop sending me postcards!" I looked at Gerald, he was an introvert, and I could relate to that. I had just found my family, and I realised how much this brother of his meant to him. I felt that I could not be the one to stand in the way of Gerald's happiness. As for Sam, surely we would hardly ever see him. I didn't want to be the awkward one to stand out against Gerald, and his plans for the future. "Yes, we can give it a go. But if Sam causes any trouble, Martin will be well within his rights to terminate your stay in the cottage."

Gerald jumped to his feet, his grin so wide that I thought it would split his face. He pumped Jim's hand, he stroked the animals, very clumsily as he was unused to them. To their credit they seemed to understand that and suffered his clumsy pats. "Thank you. Thank you. Thank you so much Daisy." The tears threatened to flow again, and with a skip he reached the front door, and raced off to see Martin.

"I'm not sure about this, but I hadn't the heart to say no," I mumbled.

"You never know," mused Jim a thoughtful look crossing his face, "a tough guy like Sam may well be welcome and handy in some circumstances. During my time, we used all sorts of people to help us in our investigations."

I returned to the kitchen carrying the mugs. That was the most revealing comment Jim had ever said about his previous life and work. Trouble is, it seemed to put the seal of approval on having a musclebound thug in our gang. This was getting ridiculous. How could Jim accept him after Sam had shot him? I realised that there was something calculating about Jim when it came to getting results. Any investigation we undertook, there was no need to follow rules, not according to Jim! I assumed it was from his spy days. Or was it something inherent in Jim himself?

CHAPTER THIRTY ONE

Wisteria cottage was set back from the lane. I got out of the car and stared up the lane to the scene of my ankle incident. Not healed properly even yet, it still caused pain, and sometimes throbbed when I walked. Dragging my eyes to the cottage gate I hesitated. I remembered Sheba bounding over it towards me. I followed Maggie through it however and closed it behind me. Halfway down the path I stood still. I was going no further until I was certain that Sheba was not going to be set upon me again. Violet opened the door and smiled at Maggie. Her gaze darkened when she caught sight of me behind her. This was not going to be a happy family reunion. Violet did not seem to welcome me, there was definitely animosity towards me in that look. Why? Why did she resent my presence?

"Violet, I've brought Daisy with me. You need to learn to chat with each other. Both of you will be in the same village groups and activities, and it will be awkward for the rest of us, if you are at odds. I did explain to Daisy that you were under the impression that she was that estate agent woman. Demelza told us that she explained about Daisy arriving here, and only just discovering her relationship with you and her mother. Daisy has only recently found out that she was born in Wisteria cottage. Could she see at least the lounge and back garden?" Maggie asked Violet.

For a moment Violet's hand tightened on the doorknob. She was going to slam it shut in our faces, I thought. Her gaze then came to rest upon Maggie, she relaxed her hand, stepped back, and muttered, "oh very well."

A dark hall opened out into a large kitchen. Along the hallway, doors opened out in each direction. "This is the main lounge." The door on my right was flung open. A pleasant room, it had a muddle of furniture from different eras, the fifties through to the nineties, but no later. My breath caught as I saw the formal photograph upon the wall. Without conscious thought, I walked up to it. A couple in 1940s dress stood awkwardly. She wore a suit of wartime era with a small buttonhole of flowers. He was in RAF uniform. I saw the slight resemblance between myself, Violet, and the woman in the photograph.

"Is that your mother?" Maggie had asked the words that had clung to my tongue.

"Yes, that's my mother and my uncle." Violet's stilted reply fell into a deepening silence.

I should have been listening. The words seem to flow over me and I didn't make them out at all because I was looking at the photograph. It was drawing me in, and I couldn't believe my eyes. Aware of Maggie and Violet now openly staring at me, I reached into my bag and got out my phone. I found the latest photograph of Jake and wordlessly turned it towards them. They both came up close behind me for a better look.

"Oh my goodness!" Maggie gasped as she bent forward.

"He is the absolute image of my uncle," breathed Violet.

The kitchen overlooked a garden that was neat, tidy, and obviously productive. Home-made strawberry jam and scones helped the difficult conversation. Sheba walked over towards me. I drew back onto my chair away from her. She sat down beside me and looked up at me. That huge shaggy dog I'm certain had a shamefaced look on her face, and she proffered a paw. Nervously I took it and shook it extremely gently. Sheba took it back, then cast an accusing look at Violet, and slumped down beside me with her head on my foot and gave a sigh.

"You'd better come with me and show her the photograph." Violet said.

"Better still Daisy, could Jake come back to see his grandmother?" Maggie suggested.

There was the unspoken thought between us. My mother was in her nineties. Time was not on her side. Seemingly fit old ladies could suddenly fade away and die. And he was only a short drive away compared to his previous Australian journey.

"I promised mother that I would go in about three o'clock this afternoon," said Violet.

"I'll ring him right now," I said.

A quick chat with Jake and he was on his way. Lisa's father was doing well, a broken arm, a very sore head and lots of bruises. He was very fortunate. They had picked him up earlier that morning and Jake could leave them. Lisa could drive her father's car so they would not be left without transport.

Jake arrived in time, and we piled into the SUV and went to pick up Violet. When we stopped outside Wisteria cottage, Jake got out and shook hands with his aunt. For a moment, they stared at each other. I didn't realise that I had been holding my breath until a smile of genuine warmth crossed Violet's face, and I let out a breathy gasp.

"You are so like the photo of my..." Here Violet stopped for a moment and turned to give me a small smile "... our uncle. Jake, come on in for a quick moment and I'll show you the photo. It will take a minute only."

"That went well Daisy," Maggie turned to me and smiled.

"Yes, I'm surprised and very grateful to you for bringing me this morning. Both you and Jim were correct, Violet and I had to be civil with each other. I still can't understand why she resented my arrival so much. But it's working out far better than I ever expected."

The door was closed and locked behind Violet, and she took her place beside Jake. We were going to the care home to visit my mother again. A lot had changed since my last visit there. I was apprehensive, this time not for myself, but for Jake. It had been a lot for him to take in, not only a new aunt but now a grandmother. I could only hope her reception of him would be far better than the one I received!

CHAPTER THIRTY TWO

The care home was just as I remembered from my last visit. But now I entered with my sister and my son beside me. Violet and I were not friends, not yet, but perhaps one day. We walked down the corridor to the bright cheerful room in which my mother lived. Today she was not in bed but sitting in a chair beside the window.

"She's having a good day," whispered the carer to me as she left the room.

"I'll go in first and prepare her for meeting her grandson." Violet smiled as she looked at her nephew, Jake.

After a few moments, Violet signalled to us to enter the room. My mother sitting upright in the chair had a beaming smile for Jake.

"At last! What took you so long? I expected you to visit me sooner Jake." A fragile hand, the blue veins pulsing beneath the papery skin was stretched out towards Jake. Gently he took the frail hand in his calloused sunburned one, cradling it gently in case he broke anything. She pulled him closer. "Let me look at you! Just as I imagined. You are the image of my brother, even to his smile. My darling brother was a pilot in the RAF. He was shot down and we never did get his body. How I missed him." The old lady sank into a reverie, obviously her thoughts were in the past. We sat silent, respecting her deeply felt emotions.

After a few moments she roused herself and turned towards Jake with an indignant expression upon her face. "Why did you make me wait so long? Violet please go into the dressing table drawer and remove the small box." The box was placed in her lap and she took a small key from the purse beside her and unlocked the box. This ceremony took some time with her shaking hands. We all watched in silence. An envelope was in the box. Obviously old, it had written in spidery writing on it, *For my Grandson.*

"This is for you, it's been waiting for you for so many years. I do hope you love it. It belonged to your grandfather and his father before him. It was always passed down the male line, so neither my twins Violet, nor... Daisy could inherit."

Jake took the envelope and held it in his hands. Silence fell upon the room, none of us knew what to say.

It was Violet who spoke first. "Mum, how did you know you had a grandson? And what is to be passed down the male line? It's the first I've heard of it."

The wrinkled face creased in disapproval as she looked at Violet. "I knew when he was born." To our utter astonishment she gave Jake's birthdate. The wrinkled face sparkled with mischief, eyes bright with amusement at our faces. "The second sight they call it. Demelza has it. You Violet sadly have none, it passed you by." She paused for a moment and then looked straight at me. It was the first time

198

she had looked straight at me full in the face. I stared back, unwilling to back down from this assault upon me. "What about you Daisy? Have you met her yet? Sensed her presence? Or have you smelt her perfume?" The voice was sharp and the question was a determined attack from the old lady.

At my start of surprise, a delighted chuckle broke from her lips. "At least one of my daughters is psychic. So Daisy, you must be my daughter after all." A frail hand was stretched out towards me. For the first time in my adult life I held my birth mother's hand. The contact between us was somehow electric and powerful, despite the fragility of the claw like hand.

Jake held up the envelope. "Thank you. Do I call you grandma? Shall I open it now?"

"Call me Gran Jake. No, take it home with you. Give me a kiss before you go. I'm tired now. I only waited to see you. All these years I knew I had to see you, you are so like your uncle and your great grandfather. Now I can leave in peace." Jake gave her a gentle kiss, and she clung to his hand and for a long moment searched his face. "So like him, his image." Her hand was then stretched out again to me. "Daisy, thank you for bringing my grandson to me. I wish there had been more time to get to know you and Jake. But I finally met you both and can see my twin girls together." The hands dropped onto her lap and she gave us all a searching look, as if committing us to memory. "Go now. I'll sleep happier now than for many a long year. Violet, you've been a wonderful daughter, give me a kiss before you go."

Silently we made our way out to the SUV. "Well Jake?" Maggie asked him. She had waited for us in the SUV.

"She was gorgeous, old and wrinkled but so bright. She knew of my birthday and had even got a letter prepared for me. How did she know that?"

With his long legs, Violet and I had given him the front seat. He turned around and looked at Violet, "how did she know about me?"

"I don't know how she knew. I knew that I had a twin sister, but never knew that she had a child until this morning. I didn't know that I was an aunt."

"Your grandmother is psychic Jake. Just like Demelza and now your mum," said Maggie. "Your Mum sees or smells the Lady that walks around the Priory kitchen. Don't deny it Daisy! You asked about her perfume, and we can see your eyes follow her about the room."

I sat quietly. To be honest, I really didn't know what to think. My mind was overburdened, there was so much that had happened so quickly and with such momentous ramifications.

Jake turned the envelope over and over in his hand. For a while the silence was tangible. Over and over his fingers turned the envelope. Then they stopped and he felt the envelope.

"There is something in here, an object. Shall I open it?"

"It's addressed to you, so you'd better open it." Violet said.

Jake still fingered the envelope. "To my grandson. How did she know? And what did she mean by the second sight? I don't understand it."

"Never mind all that, open it!" I urged him. We were all as anxious as he to find out what was in it.

A decisive rip along the top and a key tumbled out onto his lap. Then Jake shook the envelope and a business card followed the key. "A key, it looks like a door key. Not a creepy old one like you see in films. It's just an ordinary door key. This business card is for a firm of solicitors and it says on the back. *Contact Mr Perkins*. What does it mean? Why do I have to contact this man?"

I thought of the remarks Violet had made when she thought I was after the inheritance. Was this the inheritance? Had it been passed over to Jake? What had he inherited?

"What do I say? When shall I ring?" Jake was still fingering the key. We were now on the top of Bodmin moor and were about to drop down towards the Priory. Maggie pulled into a layby, stopped the SUV, and just looked at him.

"Yes Maggie, you're right. I will ring now and find out what's it all about."

After Jake's request for Mr Perkins, a

receptionist put him through. "I have just been to visit my Gran." Here, Jake paused as the word Gran passed over his lips for only the third time in his life. He gave me a fleeting smile. "She gave me a key, and your card and name." Jake listened for a while, then finished the call. "I have an appointment at five with Mr Perkins, and Mum, he wants you to come as well."

I stared at Jake. What did it mean? If Cleo hadn't broken that picture frame, none of this would have happened. I would never have come to Bodmin Moor, never have met my sister or my mother. Perhaps I might even have ended up in a bungalow beside Elsie after all. "If Cleo hadn't..." I began..

"Cleo can have a special treat from me when we get back to the Priory," promised Jake.

"Better hold off on that promise, you don't know yet what you've inherited!" Maggie warned.

"Very true Maggie, but we'll know what it's all about at five o'clock."

The others at the Priory greeted us with anxious smiles. Jake told them all the details especially the second sight remarks from his Gran. I watched him with amusement mingled with pride. The cavernous kitchen even on a sunny day, with the sun streaming in through the windows, still had shadowy corners. A movement in one of them caught my eye. She walked towards me, smiling, her hand outstretched. The dogs all stood staring at her, hair on end, and as one they moved away from that approaching figure. Cleo, who had joined us yet again stood in a defiant cat pose, her tail straight and erect, the fur on her arched back stiffly on end. A low keening noise broke from her, an otherworldly sound that echoed around the kitchen and eerily matched the moment.

The Lady gave an amused glance at the cat. "It's almost full circle now Daisy. Your mother has passed it all on to you. You always smell my perfume, and sometimes you see my shadow. Now I welcome you fully into the Shades of the Priory. Take heed of what I will tell you. I, and I alone can keep you and yours safe. Evil lurks within the Priory itself. Not all wish you joy in your inheritance. Remember Daisy, always heed my words." She faded away and was gone. Cleo shook herself and jumped onto the stool, the one that she had claimed for her own. She glared at the space where the Lady had stood and gave me an accusing look before settling down. The dogs returned to their baskets.

"She's gone?" Jim said.

"You saw her? Did anyone see her? Did you at least smell her perfume? Please someone say you..." My voice tailed away, hope faded that someone had also witnessed the appearance of the Lady. Heads shook in denial. I slumped back onto my chair. Only me, why was it always only me?

"Did she speak to you?" was the excited request from Sheila.

"Yes she spoke, she warned me of evil within the Priory. Only she can save us. I must follow her commands because not everyone is pleased at my inheritance."

"Oh, spooky," breathed Sheila. Then she thought for a moment, "what inheritance?"

"I don't know, it doesn't make sense." I replied.

"Ha, this sounds like an old black-and-white film, and a bad one at that!" Jim scoffed.

"We saw the animals react to her presence, and I thought I could smell the rose perfume," whispered Maggie, as if fearful the Lady would object to her remarks.

"I smelt lavender, and Cleo really did not like her, did she?" Sheila said, stroking the cat and smiling at the loud purrs and the little head bumping against her hand.

"I smelt lavender," admitted Martin.

"Okay, I think I smelt rose and even saw a faint shadow," was a grudging admission from Jim. "Yes, all right I admit it, but it doesn't mean I like it. I've never believed in the paranormal or supernatural, thought it all nonsense, but now in this Priory kitchen, I just don't know." Jim spread his hands out in a rare gesture of helplessness.

"It's the Priory Jim. Strange unexplained things happen here because of its antiquity," said Maggie.

Sheila picked up the key from the table, where Jake had laid it down. "So it's this afternoon appointment where you'll find out what this key opens. I think it's going to be something really good, really special Jake."

CHAPTER THIRTY THREE

Jake and I entered the solicitors building just before five o'clock. On the main street of the town centre, it was a Victorian building of dark forbidding stone. Directly from the pavement the stone steps led into a tiled lobby. The heavy oak door was ajar, and the grand hall was tiled with a wrought iron staircase rising up in ornate splendour to several floors above. Each door leading from the hall had brass plaques and names, with the professions and degrees proudly embossed upon them.

"This one Mum," Jake walked over and knocked at the oak door with Colin Perkins, upon it. We entered when the door was buzzed open into an inner hall, and a large room beyond.

"Come in, come in. My PA is off today, so just come straight through."

I had expected a dusty room with files and legal books piled up everywhere. Behind the huge desk I expected an elderly gentleman, with huge glasses perched on the long nose. Okay, someone my age, and looking it! When would I ever learn? Stereotypes are not only wrong, but when we have them fixed firmly in our minds, we end up being confounded by the reality. A young man rose to his feet, of athletic build, with a tanned face and a buzzcut, and stylish shirt open at the neck, and smart trousers. We sat down opposite him, and he resumed his seat, moving folders about on the desk. It was a large desk, and it was an old desk. He may have been young and modern, but the room conformed to the building itself, with ancient portraits and antique furniture. The electronic gadgets upon his desk were not antique though, they were obviously state-of-the-art.

"Have you brought the certificates?"

The folder I carried was soon opened, and the papers it contained passed over towards him. They were quickly read through, and he made the occasional note on the pad beside him. They were neatly folded and passed back to me.

"Firstly Jake, I see you have the key." He smiled at the key placed on the desk in front of him. "I never thought I'd see this day come. It's great to meet you and see you continue this traditional family ritual. On your grandfather's side, this property has always been handed down from son to son. The cottage in St Clether is left over from an original farm. The land was sold off and only this cottage and several acres remain. As luck would have it... I mean you!.. Not the only tenant! Oh dear, that came out all wrong. She went into a home a few months ago, so it's now empty and available." Colin Perkins smiled at Jake's astonishment.

"This actual key is to a cottage with acres of land?" Jake spoke each word clearly and distinctly, as if by doing so he could grasp the meaning. "I have now inherited a cottage and land from a grandfather I never knew existed?"

"Yes, it's a pretty one, in quite decent repair. Our firm has seen to that over the years, but the decorations inside are sadly dated, and needing modernisation. As for the garden, I'm afraid it's completely overgrown. The old lady refused to have anybody do it and refused all our offers to update inside the cottage, although it's perfectly habitable. It's legally transferred over to you, your grandmother arranged that by phone. In fact, I visited her this afternoon after your visit, to get her signature on all the legal documents required by the estate. Your grandmother is well aware of her age and fragility and wanted everything legally signed immediately. A very clever and intelligent woman, she has determination and a great deal of charm."

"Have I got this correct? I hear what you're saying, but I can't believe it. Do I really now own a cottage and land?" Jake was astonished at this, and so was I. Like two goldfish we sat staring open mouthed at the young man giving us this unbelievable news.

"Yes, you own a cottage, it's yours now, everything has been done legally. You can move in tomorrow if you like. Now Mrs..."

"Call me Daisy please." I interrupted him. Since my divorce I hated being called by my married name. But to be honest, I thought the change of name legal stuff would be far too complicated for me to undertake to revert to my maiden name. I sat on the edge of my seat, my hands were twisting nervously. What was I about to hear? Any recognition of my true identity, my birth right would be wonderful. Or would it be something unpleasant for me try to live with, in this new incarnation of my life?

"Well Daisy, as you know you are one of twins. According to your mother, you were born first, and that makes you the eldest girl. I am now going to read out to you the actual written words of your grandmother." Here he paused, shuffled his papers and with a nervous gulp continued speaking, "and according to your grandmother, you will have inherited the psychic abilities that are passed down through the maternal generations. This should be worn by you at all times, it is a talisman that....er.... protects you against all evil ones." The last words he said as quickly as possible, as if pleased to get them over with. Colin opened a drawer, brought out a jewellery box, and pushed it across the desk.

I opened it. The small gold chain lay on dark blue velvet, and ornate gold work surrounded a stone which hung on the chain. It was ancient work, and despite its simplicity it was heavy in my hand. The stone glowed and glittered as a ray of the fading sun glanced through the window and lit upon it. The box was clutched tightly in my hand as we stood up and said our farewells. Jake still had the key, but also had a new ring of keys, along with a leather folder of property deeds, and even manuals about the appliances contained within the cottage. Colin saw us out, shook hands with us, and told us to get in touch if we had any problems.

Silently we walked to the van. We both climbed in and sat there. We both looked down at our new possessions. Jake clutched the bundle of keys, resting on top of the folder with intermittent expressions crossing his face, one moment happiness and delight, the other astonishment and disbelief. He was finding it hard to come to terms with his new-found fortune and family. I looked down at the jewellery box in my hand. The monetary value of it meant nothing to me. It was the recognition, the recognition of me, of who I was. This was my birth right, I was a family member and I belonged.

"Did that happen? Do I really own a cottage? And do I have legal deeds and all this stuff? It's all mine? It's fantastic mum! Lisa and I were looking for any ropey old rental property, and even a caravan for the winter. And now! Now we have a cottage and land!"

"You haven't seen it yet. It may need a lot of work doing to it," I warned him.

"That doesn't matter, it's mine, my very own place. I don't care what state it's in. I'll fix anything that needs doing and enjoy doing it. Wait till I tell Lisa! But first we must go to the fish shop and get Cleo a reward. Do you realise if you hadn't taken in that rescue cat we would never have found our family and I would never have inherited this cottage. Our good fortune is all thanks to Cleo!"

The excitement with Jake and his inheritance had left me exhausted. My sleep broken with uneasy dreams. They shouldn't have been, I had met my sister and my mother, and been accepted by my family, Jake was going to be settled and living near to me. I should have slept well, everything seemed to be going well. Was that the problem? Why did I think that everything was going far too well. Why did I feel that there would be a problem? Was something bad going to happen in our future?

CHAPTER THIRTY FOUR

The next morning was clear and bright. We had finished breakfast, and I went back to my cottage for Flora. Today was the great day. Sheila was going for the longest trip yet in her all-terrain mobility scooter. It was unusual in having five wheels, which gave an added stability. Flora and I arrived outside the empty stable in which Sheila was housing the scooter.

"Daisy, here are water bottles, and scones, and cheese sandwiches for you, and ham sandwiches for Sheila," said Maggie handing me a package.

I stared down at the package in dismay. "It's only a short walk. We are only going to try out the scooter. It's only a short walk. We won't need all this food!" I repeated.

"Sheila's planning on being away all morning. So I made up a mid-morning break for both of you. She is determined that it should be a real expedition. Just put it in your bag and eat what you can."

I nodded, and after thanking Maggie, put the package inside my large Kipling shoulder bag. Maggie hurried back to the Priory to look for Sheila, whilst Flora and I stood waiting.

"Sorry to keep you waiting Daisy. Lottie's been a pickle when I tried to get her harness on," muttered Sheila. She had rushed out of the Priory with the tiny dog, keeping her face turned away from me. The little dog raced towards Flora barking excitedly. I didn't say a word. Sheila didn't look at me at all but fiddled with the large bag she was carrying. She knew that I would be horrified at her bringing Lottie along with her. "Didn't have time to empty all the stuff out of this bag. Still got all the paraphernalia I had in it, when I visited the grandkids yesterday. I found all these wonderful things on eBay, and I thought the kids would have great fun with them. They were so cheap because it's not Halloween and it was all leftover stock. Then I thought why worry about emptying the bag out. I'm not carrying it!" She plonked the bag down into the mobility scooters front basket. A blanket followed, "for Lottie in case she gets tired." Sheila then stood back and gazed admiringly at her scooter. "Isn't it great? It's not like an old lady type scooter at all!" She reached forward and took a duster out of the basket on the front and went round the scooter giving it a final polish.

Maggie, standing beside me, exchanged smiles with me. You couldn't be mad at Sheila for long. Her enthusiasm and excitement in every new experience was infectious, and heart-warming. Her age was no barrier, nor her disability, to enjoying and tackling every new experience she could find.

"How am I going to cope with these two dogs? Neither of them are properly trained." I muttered under my breath to Maggie. We watched Sheila get started, and she did a nifty manoeuvre out of the stable garage.

Both dogs sat side by side, their paws, I'll swear were neatly folded, as they stared up at me. Maggie pointed to them and laughed. "They're trying so hard to be good for you. Lottie loves Flora so much, I'm sure she will follow her lead." At her remark Maggie dissolved into giggles, "her lead, that's funny..."

I waved a hand at her. "Very funny! Wish me luck. Send out a search party if we don't get back for lunch!"

I had to admit, grudgingly of course, that Lottie was being good. Her tiny legs kept pace with Flora, and she clung to the other dogs side. Unusually for Flora, she neither dashed to the end of her extendable, nor ran round in circles. It was almost as if she was showing Lottie how to behave. She walked sedately along beside me, checking constantly that the tiny dog could keep up. They did look sweet together, Flora a fluffy mop headed mongrel, and Lottie a sleek brown haired miniature Dachshund, trotted along beside me obviously enjoying their walk.

"Isn't this great! It's such a lovely morning. I can go so much further now than I could ever walk." Sheila's smile was broad, and her white curls I'll swear bounced in delight. Warmly wrapped up against the cold, with a bright pink bobble hat which she had knitted, together with her long scarf in pink, with sparkling tinsel type glitter through it. I looked enviously at it, perhaps she could do a matching set for me in lime green, orange or purple. I followed along behind her, my thoughts rambling along with us.

"Yes Sheila, it really is great!" I finally replied. And it was. The cold frosty night had left patches of white sparkling remnants in the shadows. Glistening cobwebs hung garland like from bushes and trees. The sun's weak warmth was enough for steam to rise in clouds from hedges and banks, adding to Bodmin Moors mystical feel. I smiled at the older woman whose joy and delight was so obvious and so infectious. "Yes, it's a truly wonderful morning." Her returning smile was radiant, and the wrinkles seemed to vanish from her face, leaving the enthusiasm and joy of a young girl.

"This path is easy enough for my scooter, except where the horses hooves have left ruts. But I'm managing to go around those. Along the river is such a scenic path, with the hills and trees up on the skyline. I love living here, don't you Daisy? You are happy here? You have settled down with us all? You won't leave us will you?" An intent searching look was directed towards me. I realised with a sudden warmth that Sheila really was worried that I might move away. It was a new experience to find that I had friends who wanted nothing from me, just wished that I might be happy, and to be living near to them. Elsie, looking back on my relationship with her, had been demanding, and I realised that she had used me without giving me anything in return.

There are two people in life I remembered reading, one is a radiator, the other a drain. If you have a drain who leaves you exhausted tired and miserable, that is no friend. Search out those who give you joy, pleasure and are eager to help you in any way. Sheila was definitely a radiator!

"Yes Sheila, I love it here. I have settled here," I reassured her. "Now I've discovered my sister and my mother live close by, why would I ever leave? Jake, now moving down to the cottage, makes everything perfect for me."

The ruined cottages had been passed, and we were now on the level ground that lay below the hillside road. Ahead of us I saw the car debris, some still left from the thwarted attempt on our lives. I felt uneasy. It had gone quiet. Horse riders had passed us earlier, followed by an enthusiastic birdwatcher festooned with cameras, who had trotted by with a cheery greeting. But that had been some time ago. We had seen no one for the last hour. There was a quiet ominous feel, even the birds seem to have stilled their birdsong. Was I being fanciful? Surely we were safe enough here, we had not gone as far as the shooting incident the other day. I had made sure of that. So why did I feel so uneasy? I felt the hairs on the back of my neck stand up as if I was being watched.

"Shall we stop here for a moment Daisy? I think it's far enough for Lottie."

"Yes, I was about to pick her up anyway. Too long a walk is bad for a pup, and she has such tiny little legs." I put Lottie into the basket. Surprised more than worried, she settled down happily, looking about her from the new vantage point.

"Shall we go back now?" I asked, seating myself on a fallen log. A quick rest and then I would suggest we returned. All the joy on our walk had gone. Now all I could think of was returning as quickly as possible to the Priory. The sun had taken the frost off it, and I sank down with relief, after I had checked for bugs. "I think we've gone far enough."

"Yes I think you have. You've gone too far poking your nose into our business!" Came the harsh voice behind me.

CHAPTER THIRTY FIVE

The harsh voice came from behind me. The look of dismay upon Sheila's face before I turned round told me that this was no friend. Ferret Face stood behind us with a shot gun pointed at Sheila. Dishevelled, he stood there staring at us. Unshaven, he wore a too large, ancient Barbour jacket wrapped round him, and held in place with string, and his jeans hung dirty and ragged. His face was thin to the point of emaciation, and his eyes glittered with malice. I realised that he was either a very heavy drinker, or on drugs. There was a frightening lack of stability about the man. He looked on edge and finding us had obviously made him nervous.

"You lot are just too damn nosy. Dead set on finding the puppy farm aren't you?" His raucous laugh was loud and mocking. Startled crows in the nearby trees rose in protest and flew around us with screeching cries.

Slowly I rose from the log and walked over to stand beside Sheila. I placed a hand on her shoulder. "We are going back now. This was the only level path for Sheila to try out her new mobility scooter. We just passed a hiker and there were two horsewomen earlier on the path. This is a well-used path and..."

"Shut up! Shut up! You were spying on us. That's what you are always doing. Dead set on finding the puppy farm, ha ha!" This remark he repeated, finding it exceedingly funny. I didn't know why he found it so funny. Perhaps I was better off not knowing. His laughter was slightly hysterical and his face had a callous sneering look of satisfaction.

"How can I harm you? How can an old woman out for a short ride on her mobility scooter possibly harm you?" Sheila said this in a pathetic voice.

I glanced sharply at her. Sheila never called herself old. Normally she was furious if anyone even hinted at her age. What was she doing? She was obviously up to something.

"Nearly ninety years old, what harm can I do anyone?" Her voice wavered and she sank down into herself, trying to make herself look shrunken and frail.

For a moment he paused. Was he going to let us go? I kept quiet. Sheila put forward a great argument. I was not going to complicate matters. Then he made up his mind.

"Move, both of you. Dead set on finding that puppy farm. You'll see it all right, and then you'll both be dead!" His harsh grating laugh echoed round the valley. The crows rose up again in protest.

Flora was tired now, and I picked her up and cuddled her as I walked beside Sheila. Flora was a sensitive dog, and she knew something was wrong. Her puppy warmth was welcome, as I cuddled her close to me. Those ominous words of the guy with the gun had chilled me to the bone.

We trudged down the path, joining that

rutted track we had seen on the satellite pictures. The path was obvious now that we had reached it, the tracks were well used and showed that it had been heavy lorries not just light traffic. This was where those delivery lorries had been unloaded. Depositing their goods, they had turned. And left without ever seeing the final destination of the boxes. A tarpaulin covered with bracken lay beside the path. No wonder the satellite pictures did not show these preparations for the traffic and unloading. Partially covered paving slabs made a base. Obviously some goods were dumped here, covered by the green tarpaulin, until Ferret Face took them... Where? At that moment I couldn't care less where they went. All I wanted was for myself, Sheila, and the puppies to get back to the Priory. The man stopped and motioned us to stay put. He reached into his jacket and pulled out an old-fashioned walkie-talkie. That took care of the poor mobile signal in the valley I thought. My heart sank as I realised there would be little chance of us contacting the others at the Priory.

Sheila with a sneaky movement reached into her bag. She caught my eye and winked at me. Her hand dropped to her side and a brightly coloured bead fell from it. Looking away quickly, I suppressed a grin. Sheila was laying a trail just like Hansel and Gretel, but not with breadcrumbs but with beads. Both she and her granddaughter Rosie were into bead making. Yesterday Sheila had spent the day with her grandchildren. Perhaps not having time to sort out her bag was going to be an asset for us.

"I got those two old biddies here boss." Even standing apart from him we could hear the infuriated yells coming down the walkie-talkie. "What else could I do? They were coming along nosing about as usual, they had nearly reached our delivery spot." Silence from him as he stared at us, whilst listening to his boss. "Don't worry boss. Either the old quarry or those couple of mine shafts should solve the problem for good. Yes, we'll get rid of them first thing at dawn. Okay boss." He placed the walkie-talkie back in his jacket and walked towards us. "You old biddies wanted to see the puppy farm. You got your wish. Not only will you get to see it, but it's also going to be the last thing you do see. Now move."

Our way was indicated by the shot gun as he waved it down the path. Before moving I weighed up our options. Should I tackle him now? Could I take the gun off him? Was I strong enough? He was a weedy guy behind that gun.

"Come on Daisy," Sheila's voice was a warning one. Her look said, don't do it, and she gave a slight shake of her head. "Put Flora in the basket beside Lottie. It'll save you carrying her."

I knew what she meant. Holding a dog and launching an attack on a man with a gun was foolish to put it mildly. Flora went in the basket, and Sheila gripped my hand encouragingly, before we turned off the main trail. Ferret Face was now behind us, shouting directions. Once we had gone past that initial turnoff from the trail, we found a road which had been cunningly concealed by branches laid upon it. This road was again in good condition. Heavy vehicles had obviously traversed it, so making easier going for Sheila's scooter. Then we came to a stone rockface. Ferret Face came round from behind us and walked towards the rocks. He bent down behind a large boulder and seemed to press a tiny lever at its base. There was a grinding machinery noise, and stone slid upon stone and part of the cliff face slid back.

"Wow! That's cool!" Sheila cried out in astonishment.

Ferret Face grinned at us. Not a pretty sight, the toothless smile was a travesty of humour. I preferred his scowl. "Never find this would you?" he scoffed. He walked in, and then signalled for me to follow, and then Sheila. As she wheeled the mobility scooter up the ramp, a beautifully laid concrete one I noticed, Sheila dipped into the bag yet again. This time there were quite a few beads dropped. My only hope was that the bad guys wouldn't notice them, and the good guys would find them. I didn't only hope, I prayed!

CHAPTER THIRTY SIX

Our footsteps echoed, and Sheila's scooter wheels made a shushing sound over the rock floor, as we entered the rocky entrance. The yellowish water of the stream that had been alongside the path, gurgled beside us as we walked further into the huge tunnel. A large cavern opened out around us. Was it man-made or natural? I did not have the knowledge that would have told me. There were a couple of narrow exits at the back of the cavern. One had a large padlock on the door, the other as I walked further into the cavern was obviously a dead-end. I remembered Gerald telling me about the early miners and realised that the piles and ridges of soil alongside the path on our way to the cavern, had been what Gerald had called tailings. Those early miners looking for metals, copper, tin, and even gold had sluiced the streams and piled up the debris. Hundreds of years of exposure had covered them with soil and grass. I touched the wall beside me and could still see the pick marks made all those years ago, by miners in their search for precious metals. There were colours in some of the rocks, and there was obviously machinery at the end of the cavern. Was it to dig out those colours which were perhaps precious metals? So interested in my surroundings, I had barely noticed what lay before me. It was Sheila's exclamation of horror that brought me literally down to the ground. This was the puppy farm. This is what we had been searching for. We had found it, but we were now incarcerated beside the wretched puppies we had been intending to rescue.

"Make yourselves at home ladies, because tomorrow you die!" Laughing in an almost manic manner Ferret Face turned away from us and walked quickly through the door mechanism. As the door slid behind him we could still hear that laugh, and his voice shouting back at us, "tomorrow you die!"

Sheila looked at her scooter, "I'm nearly out of juice, we should look for a point to plug it in for our escape." She rose and stepped off it and looked around. "It's some sort of cave, isn't it?"

"No, I think it's actually a mine. Not all of them were shafts going down into the earth. Some of the old miners used to work in the streams, then follow a vein and dig into the rock horizontally. This looks like one of those, look you can see the pick marks on the wall."

I lifted Lottie and then Flora out of the basket and walked towards Sheila. She was standing, almost sobbing as she pointed. "This is it Daisy. We found the puppy farm and it's absolutely ghastly!"

The cavernous space was divided into two parts. The far back wall had tools, equipment, and a low loader, and something that looked like a baby tractor. They were all in shadow, their shapes not easily discernible. There was however lights slung in ropes across the front of the cavern, beneath them there were pens and hutches. A table stood against one wall, piled beneath it were bags of dry dog food, and bowls. The stream ran alongside the table, which had obviously been placed there for easy access to the water. The only sound we could hear was that tinkling gurgle of the stream. A musty smell lingered in the fetid air. There were dogs in some of the pens, but most of them were empty. All those dogs that were there stared at us pathetically. Not one of them barked, whined, or showed any animation at all at our arrival.

Lottie and Flora had just sat beside us staring about them. Then all of a sudden Lottie gave a tiny bark. She raced across to a pen barking little yips of excitement. A solitary dachshund looked up, and out of the pen towards the puppy. It gave a shake of its head, and slowly rose to its feet. At first it just stared at the oncoming puppy, then with growing animation rushed towards the gate.

"That must be Lottie's mum!" Sheila went across and opened the catch. The two dogs sniffed each other. Lottie raced round and round the other dog, who stood bemused at first. We saw the growing realisation in her eyes that this was her puppy. The two sat down together and Flora joined them. We left them and wandered round exploring. After this, Sheila returned and sat upon the scooter, which she had plugged in for recharging. They had obviously managed to get an electricity connection. I'd found a couple of chairs and carried one over beside the scooter, the one that did not wobble. I sat beside Sheila. "What are we going to do?" I sighed.

"We are going to get out of here and take this lot with us!" With a large expansive gesture Sheila encompassed all the puppies and their mothers.

"Why have so many dachshunds?" I wondered aloud. I ignored Sheila's declared intention of escaping with the entire doggy lot.

"Small and easily sold. Folk are into tiny handbag dogs. That's why there are so many of the smaller dogs. There are only a couple of Cavalier King Charles Spaniel mums left. I think they've either sold a lot, or they are winding down the puppy farm."

We were startled by the noise of the cliff door moving. Whilst there was lighting, in the cavern it was dim. The afternoon sunlight streamed in towards us, making us blink in its glare. Two figures were darkly silhouetted against the light. They came towards us.

"Here they are boss. Those two old ladies who keep nosing into our affairs." Ferret Face pointed to us. His voice was shrill and nervous.

The taller man entered behind him. The sun behind him made his dark shadow spread out towards us, engulfing us both in sudden darkness. I shivered. The evil in this man clung to him. Ferret Face was obviously frightened of him.

"Feed the dogs now." Ferret Face rushed to the table and began clanging metal bowls, filling them with rattling dry dog food. Water was splashed into other bowls, which were dumped in each pen. He said nothing, ignoring each dog just automatically placing the bowls beside them.

"You have been a nuisance to me." The man's voice was soft, and purred gently almost cat like, which seemed strange in a puppy farm. "I never tolerate nuisances. I remove them from my path."

"I suppose Alice was a nuisance!" Sheila blurted out.

"Yes, Alice did become a nuisance. She no longer bothers me." The voice was relentless in his certain assurance of getting his own way, and the callous manner he had of obtaining it. Shivers ran up my spine. I've met evil before, but somehow this man embodied an evil so great it overwhelmed me. Almost overwhelmed me.

"You didn't send us over that cliff though did you?" Sheila attacked him again.

Even with his face in the shadow, I could see it darken with fury and his hands clenched into fists at his sides. "That was a foolish mistake by my man. He paid dearly for that."

"With his life!" sneered Sheila.

"I do not make foolish mistakes. This time I will carry out the deed myself. I'm sorry ladies, but there will be no customary last meal for you. Unless you join the puppies in their food. Tomorrow morning at dawn, we will escort you to a mineshaft. Deep, dark and extremely well hidden, it will be a fitting grave for you nosy busybodies." The calm purring voice rose until he was almost screaming the last words at us. Ferret Face was casting frightened glances towards his boss. He was terrified of this man. That did not bode well for us!

"Enjoy yourselves with the pups." He began to walk towards the entrance then caught sight of Sheila's large bag. "What's in there? Phones won't work here. What's in that bag?"

Sheila stiffened. She didn't want that man looking into her bag. Whatever she had in there, she wanted to keep it. I could see her mind working, then I caught a little lift of her lips and she glanced at me. Oh no! Sheila was up to something, I knew that look. We were in enough trouble as it was. Was she going to get us into more trouble?

"You've no toilet in here. I've had to put my used incontinence pads in my bag. I will open it if you want to check them out." Sheila began to open the bag, pulling the zip back just a short way and offering the bag to him.

He backed hastily away, and almost ran for the entrance. "See you both tomorrow," were his parting words. And he was gone, Ferret Face with him and the door screeched and noisily closed again behind them.

"Incontinence pads? Used ones?" I stared at Sheila in astonishment.

"Would you look in my bag after I told you that?" Sheila asked me with a broad grin on her face.

"No! No way!" Was my instant reply.

"Exactly, I reckoned that a man would feel even stronger about that."

"But you don't..." I began.

"No thankfully. That's one of the hazards of old age I have not encountered. I'm hungry, let's eat whatever Maggie put in our bag before we get going on our escape plan."

"Our escape plan?" I muttered glancing towards the cliff door and the huge locking mechanism. How the hell were we to get out of this pickle?

CHAPTER THIRTY SEVEN

Maggie had packed far too much for a mid-morning snack. "Thanks Maggie, thank goodness you packed too much as usual." Sheila said as she began eating her ham sandwich. "Come on Daisy, you must eat your lunch, you'll need all your energy and strength later."

The crusty home-made roll and the local Cornish cheese had been in my hand for several minutes. I had stared at it without even seeing it. The overwhelming feeling of helplessness that had engulfed me, had taken my appetite away. No phone signal meant that we couldn't contact the others. No one had ever found this mineshaft/cavern over the many years it had been searched for. Sheila's bead trail was the faintest hope of all, it could be missed so easily. Sheila's optimism and enthusiasm for an escape seemed ridiculous to me. There was no way we could get out. Even if we somehow managed it, we had to go past the farmhouse. Sheila's scooter made a noise, but there was no way we could get back without it. I hated to admit it, but I really felt that this was going to be my last day on earth.

"Daisy eat up!" Sheila's voice broke into my thoughts. I ate. "There are fewer dogs here than I would have thought. There's only about twelve in all. Let's get those movable fence things and make a huge ring for them all. Flora and Lottie can go and join them. Then we can look at what's going on at the back of the cave."

Sheila led the way towards the back of the cavern. Machinery and tools were placed against the granite walls. There was a damp musty smell the further we walked into the cavern. The shadows were oppressive, and the drips of moisture down the walls gave an eerie background noise which unsettled me further. A stout wooden door locked further entry down another shaft. "Do you think they have been looking for gold and maybe found it?" Sheila said.

"I don't know Sheila. Whenever Gerald told me about the mining, I actually switched off. You know how boring he can get. Maybe there is gold down here."

"Daisy, this machinery is dusty from disuse. It doesn't seem as if it's been used in a while. Maybe the goldmining didn't pan out," Sheila chortled, "get it? Didn't pan out."

I smiled automatically. Sheila was trying to make light of the situation. The least I could do was to go along with her crazy idea of an escape. At least that was better than thinking of my imminent death!

"The goldmining isn't working, the puppy farm is just ticking over. The real reason for the secrecy and the murders must lie behind that door." The wooden door had a secure lock and a padlock for an extra security measure. Whatever was behind that door was the reason Alice had been murdered, and the reason that they now wanted us dead.

"Come on Daisy, never mind that wretched door. We've got to get our escape plan going. It's four o'clock now and must be getting dark outside. The others will be looking for us. They know which way we went, it may only be a matter of time before they find us."

"If they can, this is private property. They can hardly search all over Hilltop farm for us." I doubted very much that Jim and the others could undertake a proper search. The rule of law was such that they would be trespassing. If they could get in unseen, that would be a different matter. But could they? Then again, when did Jim ever obey the law? If he wanted to break it, I was certain he would. I thought it very possible that Tenby might well turn a blind eye to Jim's search. Or could he find a legal way of searching for us? Surely if there was one possible route to organise a legal search, Tenby would find it. With these thoughts, I felt a bit better, perhaps it wasn't hopeless after all.

Some of the puppies were mixing happily now with Flora and Lottie. The older mums were not too sure, they stayed within their original pen. It was all they knew. I watched them for a while, and then turned to look at Sheila who was rummaging in her bag.

"I'm going to paint the dogs. Daisy, you get to work and break that mechanism at the entrance."

"Paint the dogs?"

"I bought this glow paint for Ben and Rosie

to paint their two puppies for Ben's birthday party. It's non-toxic and washable, and in the USA they paint skeletons on the dogs for Halloween. It's really cool isn't it?" She brought out a spray can and put it on one side.

"Why on earth do you want to paint the dogs? I don't understand."

"Those guys are coming when it's dark to kill us. How do you think they'll feel if a load of dogs run round glowing like skeletons and with headbands. And it will confuse them if we make an earlier escape." Delving again into the bag, Sheila produced giant glowing eyeballs on headbands, specially attached to gentle elastic prepared for the birthday party children. "These look eerie when it's dark, they are fantastically spooky."

I stared down at these preparations. I wasn't sure about it at all. But I shrugged my shoulders, it couldn't hurt, and may well give us an element of surprise to escape. Sheila now expected me to break the entrance mechanism. I went to the back and returned with a metal bar and a large hammer. I went to the mechanism. I banged it a few times. I did not understand how it worked, which didn't help. I tried to prise bits off the door but couldn't manage it. Nothing worked. I sat back down on the one stable chair dropping my tools on the floor. I ached, my hands hurt, and nothing had even shifted in the slightest.

Sheila had been busy. All the dogs had a painted outline of their bodies on them. They didn't seem to mind, in fact the older mums seemed to enjoy the attention. On the table the plastic eyeballs were placed out ready to snap onto each dog. Picking up my useless tools I wandered back to the machinery against the granite wall. I stared at it all, surely I could find something that would help us escape.

"My scooter is charged up ready to go. When we get ready I'll pile the tiniest pups in my basket. The others can come with us when we escape. We'll wait till it's dark and then when we think they are asleep, I think we should go then."

"Sheila how can we take them all? I don't want to let them all loose, and how could we take them with us. They will run all over the place. It's just not practical. Surely we could come back for them, it's twelve dogs after all. And I haven't got the entrance mechanism unlocked."

"Yes, okay, I'll rethink this," muttered Sheila. She sat on her mobility scooter, the pups playing about her feet. "I'll think of something, I must. There must be some way to make sure they stay together and with us."

I watched her get busy sorting out an escape plan. Her enthusiasm put me to shame. The feeling of helplessness that had engulfed me had to be shaken off. With a renewed determination I walked up to the tools, coils of rope, and machinery. There was the low loader type of thing. As I walked up to it, I realised the keys were still in the ignition. Obviously they thought there was no need for security in the cavern. This was used to cart boxes about I felt certain. What boxes? I expect they were in that locked shaft. Never mind about that I thought to myself. The loader had two large prong things, perhaps I can use them to get rid of that door mechanism. I was unused to the controls and jerked and juddered across the uneven ground towards the entrance. I gritted my teeth and crashed into that door mechanism, again and again, trying with the prong things to pull the mechanism away from the entrance door. The grinding of the metal against metal throughout the cavern was horrendous. After a while, there was a huge clanging crash of metal. Nervously I stopped and looked round at Sheila. "Do you think they'll hear that?"

"It doesn't matter, you've done it. Daisy you sheared the lock off completely! We should be able to slide open that door and escape."

"Let's hurry, before they come to investigate the noise." I rushed to help Sheila put the puppies into the scooter basket. The larger dogs she had roped together in groups of four, gently with the soft elastic around tummies, so gently, I wondered if it would actually stay put when we set off. They all stood looking puzzled, but quietly happy. They had enjoyed Sheila's ministrations and trusted her now. The bigger ones had their eyeball headdresses, all lit up and each one of them including the smaller pups had the glow paint painted on them. She had painted fluorescent skeleton shapes on each dog, and round rings around their eyes. I put my shoulder bag in its cross body position, because I had a couple of smaller puppies stuck in there and I didn't want to jar them. I grabbed Flora and Lottie's leads, and the other ropes with the dogs attached. Nervously I followed Sheila, struggling to lead my mob of dogs as she drove out of the entrance on her mobility scooter.

CHAPTER THIRTY EIGHT

The darkness outside was impenetrable at first. It had only been dimly lit inside the cavern. Now, although it was only about five o'clock, darkness had descended onto the valley floor. Sheila had found a large torch which I was using. We began to slowly ease our way back along the path we had been marched upon earlier by Ferret Face. I followed Sheila, bringing up the rear with my mob of dogs. The dogs surrounded us in a fearful muddle.

"Wow, Sheila that is amazing!" Each dog had something upon it. Most had the glowing fluorescent skeletons painted on them, their eyes circled with huge rings. The bigger dogs had flashing LED headbands, originally meant for the children, placed around their necks. Soft elastic only, it wouldn't hurt the dogs, she had assured me. Other headbands were now lit up with giant eyeballs on stalks. It was frankly weird and unsettling. I knew what they were, but even I was astonished at the impact they had in the darkness. The elastic she had found in her bag, was gently wound round tummies to link them together. To my delight it was holding each dog in place on the rope. The dogs were all delighted at the attention and seemed to enjoy this outing.

"Pretty good Daisy! Don't they all look great?" Sheila said with pride, as she juddered along pushing the mobility scooter to its absolute limit in speed.

"Yes they look great Sheila, but this is like herding cats! They're enjoying themselves so much and are rushing around everywhere. It's hard getting them to follow me." My feet now had to be put down with great care in case there was a puppy beneath it. Or else I tripped over a twine lead with a couple of dogs on the end tethered with stretchy elastic.

We had gone a short way from the cavern, and I was beginning to have a faint flicker of hope that we might, just might, in our bizarre fashion really escape. Then I heard the voices.

"That's those old women, they must have broken out of the cavern somehow. No way they are going to escape us!" The farmhouse was set up a hill, getting its name from the hilltop it sat on. To one side of us the ground sloped up towards it. Shouts, and the noise of feet running down the hill could be heard. Trying to be quiet, I had previously urged the dogs on with hissed encouragement. There was no need for secrecy now. So I began yelling at Flora and Lottie to lead the dogs down the path to home. Flora sat still and then looked at me.

"Come on Flora, we have to get this lot home safely. We have to hurry!" Did she really nod her head at me? She jumped up on her four paws, gave a little bark towards Lottie, and set off down the path. Lottie of course followed her, and to my utter relief and bewilderment all the puppy farm dogs joined in the mad chase for home. They were gallant little dogs, unused to exercise. It must have been difficult for them, but Flora and Lottie encouraged them. When I looked at them closely, I was certain they were all laughing and loving the crazy escapade.

"What the hell!" Ferret Face appeared around the next corner of the path. Swear words, most of which I'd never heard before, issued from his mouth. As he rushed towards us a rope full of Dachshund mums tangled him up, and he fell heavily. That crash on the ground came with even more swear words. I rushed over to him and hit him hard on the shoulders with the wooden stave Sheila had given to me earlier as a makeshift weapon. He flung himself awkwardly to one side, dropping the gun he had been holding. His other arm went up to protect his head in case of a blow from me. I would have loved to clonk him on the head, but I stepped back. The rope full of dogs that had initially tripped him up, now tangled him up with themselves. There was no way he could get free without help. I bent and picked up the gun and stepped away from him. I held the gun nervously in one hand.

"Daisy, the boss man is coming. Daisy take care." Sheila warned as she pulled up her mobility scooter beside me. She was also carrying a wooden stave and couldn't resist giving the hapless Ferret Face a couple of sharp cracks with it. Then she was off her scooter and gave me a ball of twine from her capacious bag. I had trussed up Ferret Face in seconds. I moved around him and got the dogs back into a semblance of order on their rope

There was no way we could run off and escape the boss. He was too near for us to even attempt it. I stood there awaiting his arrival. "Don't come any nearer, or I will shoot." I shouted at him as he rushed towards us.

"You old bag. You'd never fire that gun. You'd be afraid of the bang!" He continued towards me. Thankfully he seemed to be unarmed. Obviously, he left the rough stuff to his men. In the light of our torch I could see the sneering look on his face. He was certain that I would meekly submit to his orders. I glanced at Sheila, and I saw her nod her head.

"Shoot him Daisy!"

"Don't come any nearer or I will shoot you!" I shouted at him. Taking a deep breath, I stiffened my shoulders, carefully placed the puppy bag behind me and lifted the gun.

"Go on then," he laughed at me, still confidently approaching me.

So I shot him. I aimed at the dirt beside his foot. I missed. I shot him right in middle of his foot! With a howl of pain he dropped to the ground. Words spewed from his lips. He had a better repertoire of swear words than Ferret Face. "You shot me, you stupid old cow. You shot me!" Those were the only words I really understood.

"Well done Daisy!" Sheila was cheering and yelling beside me. She danced around with a wild war dance! "Don't you move Ferret Face or Daisy will shoot you full of lead! As well as your boss!" She bent over the prone body on the ground and snarled it in his face. Ferret Face watched his boss writhing in agony on the ground. It had taken the last of the fight out of him. Cheers and triumphant yells erupted again from Sheila. This time Flora, Lottie and all the dogs joined in barking with her.

"That must be Sheila and Daisy!" Jim's voice echoed up the path towards us. Feet pounded along in the sudden silence that fell when we quietened the dogs. Only the moans from the boss clutching his foot could be heard. Three figures emerged from the trees down the lane. Brilliant torchlight lit up the scene. I shielded my eyes from the glare. But not before I realised how bizarre everything looked to the newcomers. One man on the floor clutching a bleeding foot, the other trussed up with a constant procession of dogs wandering all over him. Sheila was waving a wooden stick in triumph, and every dog and puppy sported a fluorescent skeleton or a headband with glowing giant eyeballs.

"Daisy! Sheila are you both all right?"

It was Jim's voice that we heard behind the flashlight. Jim, Martin, and Gerald rushed over towards us. They only gave fleeting glances to the men on the floor. Martin gave Sheila a huge hug, his grin so wide it almost broke his face. Jim grabbed me and held me at arm's length.

"You weren't shot? We heard gunfire. You're not hurt? Is Sheila hurt?" His voice was deep and ragged and was breaking as he hugged me. At my assurances that we were both unhurt, he pushed me back staring at me, and then gave me another hug. It was Flora and Lottie jumping up at Jim caused us to break away.

"Flora and Lottie! I might have guessed you'd be in the middle of it! Good gracious, what have you done to all these dogs? And what are they all doing out?" Jim said trying to pat both dogs and looking around at the same time.

Overwhelming relief flooded through me and I began to laugh. "It was Sheila and her bag. It wasn't incontinence pads after all... It was her bag..." I caught myself in time. Even I could hear the slightly hysterical note creeping into my laughter.

Martin looked around at the fluorescent dogs and shook his head. "That was a brainwave of yours Sheila. Those fluorescent beads that you dropped glowed in the dark. They made it so easy for us to follow your path."

Heavy footsteps could be heard. A large figure joined us but began cursing as he fell over a rope with several fluorescent dogs attached to it.

CHAPTER THIRTY NINE

"What the hell is going on here?" Tenby staggered, as a doggy rope tangled around his ankles. He did a nifty move, obviously from his earlier rugby playing days, and stepped over it. "Why are these dogs everywhere? What's happened here?" He came further into our view, followed by a couple of his men. "I told you to wait for us!" He pointed a finger at Jim, it wavered and dropped suddenly, as he realised that Sheila and I were in the middle of the dogs, and had Ferret Face tied up, and the boss lying wounded beside us. "You found the puppy farm Daisy." It was a statement. No congratulations, no pleasure, just a resigned exasperated tone. Then he gave a gulp as he realised that Ferret Face had a tangle of glowing pups milling about and over him.

The moans of the boss man had him over beside him in seconds. "Shot! Daisy at it again? We came to rescue the two ladies. Didn't realise we'd have to come and rescue the villains!"

"Daisy smashed the cliff entrance mechanism with a machine," exclaimed Sheila.

"Of course she did. Why did I expect nothing less." Tenby gave a sigh of resignation and shook his head.

I pointed to the dogs and puppies, milling about happily, still lit up with the huge eyeballs. "It was Sheila who painted them and thought of the fluorescent headbands to distract the men."

"And we came to rescue you both." Tenby said shaking his head at the two men, very much the worse for wear after Sheila and my efforts.

"You didn't need to, once we got the dogs sorted, we just had to haul our butts out of the cavern," said Sheila.

We all stared at her.

"She's been watching those American cop shows again. I preferred Intel. I don't like the phrase hauling her butt," whispered Martin to me.

If I only had to worry about Sheila's bad American language, that was fine by me. No more fear of attack from Ferret Face and best of all, no more puppy farm.

The policemen started to get the two men up and ready for the police cars. Jim, Martin, and Gerald began to sort out the fluorescent dogs. With a lead, or rope in each hand they managed to set off for the Priory. Sheila of course trundled along on her mobility scooter. I followed the group with Flora and Lottie. Jim had taken my bag with the two puppies, and held the rope with Lottie's mum, and another couple of dachshund mums.

"All I can think of is a long hot shower." I declared. At my words Martin, Gerald, and Jim all turned to stare at me, with looks of horror mingled with guilt upon their faces.

"What? What is it?" I asked them. Why did my longing for a hot shower cause such consternation?

"Hurry up, let's get back to the Priory. It's getting dark and cold, and we have to sort out all the puppies and the dogs. Let alone sort out these guys, and then statements." Tenby's voice boomed over us all, echoing round the valley.

It wasn't too long before we reached the Priory courtyard. Maggie rushed out to greet us all, flinging her arms first around Sheila, and then me, laughing and crying at the same time. Sheila had now got into her third wind and was busy telling the tale again and again of how she saved us. A horrified gasp broke from everyone, when they realised how close we were to being killed at dawn.

"I suppose you sat and did nothing, whilst Sheila did all the work," whispered Jim in my ear.

"Sheila did have the ideas of the fluorescent paint and the eyeballs. But I smashed the door down. It was great fun! The metal buckled and shrieked, and squealed, as I rammed it again and again. It made me feel good, as if I was getting back at them for their incarceration of us and the dogs. Now all I can think of is a long hot shower."

"Not one of you has had the courage to tell Daisy. Have you?" Demanded Maggie, her hands on hips, as she glared at the men. "Martin you tell her! It's all your fault."

Martin shuffled his feet, looked at the ground, looked at everyone, but didn't look at me.

"What's happened to my shower? No water, no electricity?" I was shaking with fatigue. And the stress of the last few hours had left me feeling weak, wobbly, and even a bit tearful.

"Well you see, it happened like this. I was so busy trying to reach Tenby, and so worried about you and Sheila, that I didn't really stop him." Martin gabbled the words. Again, without looking at me.

"Oh, for goodness sake! It's Nigel, your ex-husband has arrived." Maggie told me as she glared at Martin furiously.

"What? He came in and deliberately broke my shower?" I exclaimed in horror.

"Daisy, do stop going on about your stupid shower." Jim said to me in exasperation. He continued speaking, "Nigel, arrived at lunchtime after we realised you and Sheila were missing. Gerald and I were out searching for you, Maggie was manning the phones, and Martin was trying to explain to Tenby and the policemen which way you had gone. We were all distraught. Martin had his hands full, so don't blame him," said Jim.

This had been said with a nervous look towards me, and even Jim stared down at his feet. Why was it that all these men had to stare at their feet?

"So Martin let Nigel in to break my shower?" I queried.

"Forget your damn shower Daisy!" Jim shouted at me.

"Easy for you to say! You didn't have to sit down on the dogs bedding all afternoon. And it was stinky and dirty," was my infuriated retort.

"Martin let Nigel wait for you in your cottage, while the men searched for you. Somehow he broke your shower. He promised to look after your cat."

That noise I had vaguely heard in the background, I suddenly realised, was Cleo my cat wailing at the top of her voice. I had never heard that noise from her. She must be in pain. I rushed towards my cottage.

"He promised to look after my cat? He didn't bother to come and look for me? He hates cats, and it sounds as if Cleo hates him!"

My cottage door opened and Nigel stood there for a moment. At the sight of me he rushed towards me his arms open wide.

"Daisy! Thank goodness you're safe. I've been so worried about you, my darling Daisy!"

Sidestepping him neatly, I ran into the cottage. The cage sat in the middle of the kitchen with a furious cat yelling her head off. Opening the door, I sat down on the floor beside the cage. Cleo threw herself at me, her claws clung to my jacket, and she clambered up and round my neck. Broken hearted wails mixed with purring came from her. The others followed me into the cottage standing inside the door.

"Oh no! Your kitchen," Maggie whispered, her hand to her mouth. Dirty mugs, and glasses stood on the worktop. An empty pizza box, the dirty plate with the remains of the crust of the pizza lay beside them. The lounge had Nigel's coat and bag flung on the sofa. A newspaper, it's sheets lay scattered upon the floor, mute evidence of his search for the sports page. His shoes lay where he'd stepped out of them.

My eyes wandered around the lounge, as I turned my back on the kitchen mess. My latest painting, lay upon the dining table, set out ready for the framer. One of my best paintings, the painting had taken not only hours, but days to get it to the state of perfection required for botanical eyes. Still holding Cleo, who had taken root upon my shoulders, I walked over to the painting. A coffee mug sat on the middle of it, with a pool of coffee spread around it, over my painting. The others followed my gaze and became silent witnesses to the scene of devastation that Nigel had wrought upon my cottage, and painting in a matter of hours. Whilst I was in danger of death, he had been eating pizza, reading the newspaper, and generally causing havoc in my cottage.

"My painting!" I exclaimed.

"I see you started your little hobby again. Nice dear, very nice. Don't worry, it's only a little splash of coffee. You can always do another, got plenty of time now." Lifting the coffee mug, he wiped the pool of coffee with the back of his hand. "Oh dear, seems I've made it much worse." The sharp intake of breath from the others still clustered around the door finally registered with him. But he only looked puzzled. "What? What's the matter?"

CHAPTER FORTY

"My painting!" I stared at Nigel. Really looked at him. He looked older, the faint laughter lines from before were now deep wrinkles, with a downward petulant slant. His hair no longer cut in the former smart style, was dishevelled, greying, and getting sparse. The shirt was crumpled and faded. The trousers whose immaculate creases I'd always achieved for him, were badly ironed.

I was speechless. The rage that was boiling up inside me couldn't find words to express itself. So I stood there, exhausted, filthy, and unable to formulate the anger that hovered on my tongue. Pushing between the numerous legs at the doorway, Flora and Lottie raced into the room. They jumped up at me, then Cleo, eager to greet their friend, deliriously happy to be home again. Seeing Nigel, Flora who loved men, rushed towards him. Flora jumped up at him, with Lottie following to join in the fun.

"Get these damn dogs out of my way! First you have a yowling cat. Now you have these yapping little dogs. These have to go Daisy. All these horrible creatures have to go. No way am I living here with you and this lot! Silly yapping creature. Leave my foot alone!" Nigel drew back his foot to give Flora a kick. He caught her a glancing blow, luckily with his stocking foot. But still she yelped.

"Don't you dare kick my dog!" I didn't even recognise my own voice. I'd screamed the words in a harsh bitter tone that had erupted from within me. I was exhausted. The nervous energy after our kidnap, and our escape, had together with the physical exercise I had expanded, left me at breaking point. Maggie's snack had been hours ago, and I was running on empty. Reaching into my pocket, I drew out the small pistol I had removed from Ferret Face. I had injured the Boss with this gun from his companion, Ferret Face. When I tied him up, I had removed the gun when he had dropped it. After shooting the Boss I'd slipped it into my own pocket. And forgotten all about it in the chaos of our rescue. I pointed it at Nigel's leg. "Kick my dog again and I'll shoot you in that damned foot."

Nigel stared at me, his jaw hung open. Then he laughed at me. "You wouldn't shoot me Daisy. I know you. Ha, you wouldn't shoot anyone. You're not capable of it. In fact, you're not capable of much are you?"

His words fell into silence. That remark reminded me of the years when he belittled me, when I had felt useless to the point of stupidity. That was then. I wasn't the same person anymore. I had changed, I had grown in confidence. My experiences with my new friends had made my life enjoyable, and I was looking forward to it continuing with my newfound family and son. Nigel's nasty remarks no longer had the power to hurt me. I smiled at him, "I shot a man in the foot tonight, another one won't make any difference to me," I warned him. My hand tightened on the gun, and my finger hovered over the trigger. How I wanted to press that trigger!

"Rubbish, you can't shoot me. There's witnesses here, even a high ranking policeman. Ha, Daisy dear, don't be a silly little woman."

My finger tightened on the trigger, that patronising sneering remark almost had me shooting him. I relaxed my finger. He wasn't worth it. But then, Flora bounced towards him and nibbled his big toe. Nigel glared down at her and drew back his foot and kicked out with a vicious thrust. My shot went through his sock before he could reach her.

"You shot me! What the hell! You've gone and shot my foot. I'm bleeding! Hey, you're a policeman. You saw her, she shot me!" Nigel slumped down on the sofa and peeled off his sock. There was only a little bit of blood, the bullet had grazed his big toe only. In one way I was very relieved, and in another vicious way I wished I'd shot his big toe off. "You saw her, what are you going to do about it? Hey, you, Tenby isn't it. You saw her, Daisy shot me!"

"You kicked that dog earlier and were about to kick it again. Daisy warned you not to kick it," said Tenby. He had folded his arms and was staring down at Nigel with a blank expression on his face. Tenby was as angry as I was, I could see it in the compressed lips and clenched fists.

"Badly behaved creature, why all this fuss for a stupid dog," shouted Nigel. Massaging the toe and mopping up the little blood with a tissue, he was red in the face with fury. He looked round the group, wondering at the silent faces staring at him. No one spoke, no one moved, they all just stared at Nigel.

In quiet tones, Tenby spoke to Nigel, "that creature was originally my dog."

Nigel's face whitened, "your dog?"

Grins spread over the faces at the doorway.

Tenby turned towards me, he winked at me, and said in solemn tones, "Daisy, did you happen to accidentally discharge that gun? If you did, that was only an accident. If you wanted to discharge it yet again, that could be yet another accident. I'd be quite happy to take it from you and caution you. If you happened to accidentally get a better shot at that foot of his, well, it would just be a silly accident again. We would all vouch for it being an accident, wouldn't we?"

The smiles from the others, the emphatic nods, and murmurs of assent, made Nigel wince. "Daisy love, surely this is all a joke, I came so that we could get back together. I'd even considered living in this terrible place."

The pistol had dropped by my side. I lifted up the gun and pointed it at his foot. His other foot! "I think you had better leave, my finger is itchy on the trigger. Leave now!" Even I was surprised at the cold harsh tones of my voice. There was no arguing or pleading with me, I was going to do it if he didn't leave. Nigel's face which was already pale, flushed a sudden dark red as the realisation grew that I actually meant what I said. If he didn't leave now I would shoot him again, and everyone in that room would vouch for it being an accident.

Flora, aware of this confrontation, but at a loss as to what actually was going on, came and sat on my foot. Cleo, after my shot, had taken up a position on the window seat behind Tenby. Every so often she peered out behind his large figure. Lottie had now become aware of the threat Nigel presented to her and Flora. She gave a tiny bark of defiance up at him, and then ran towards Flora. They bumped noses, and she glanced up at me. She gave a huge sigh of relief or contentment, whatever it was, she relaxed and settled herself down on my other foot. That was it! As I stared down at the two dogs, one on either foot I realised that I had lost the battle. I had three pets now. Lottie's glance up at me had held love and complete trust in me. There was no way I could let her go to another home. For better or worse I now had three pets.

In the silence that had descended after Nigel's pointless pleading, he had begun to gather up his things. "You're making a huge mistake," he muttered as he made for the door.

"The biggest mistake I ever made, was when I married you!" I replied. He left. Tenby strode over and took the gun from me. Nigel's car started up, and I heard it drive through the courtyard archway. I knew that shot had not really hurt him. I felt nothing when he left. I was empty and felt drained of every emotion. I wanted a mug of tea and a shower. Voices suddenly seemed loud around me, and I felt very strange. The room started to move, and lights began to flash about me. "I want a shower," I muttered.

"Come on Daisy. You've reached breaking point. All this drama on an empty stomach is not good. Come on, let's get you into the bedroom." Maggie's gentle arm came round my shoulder and guided me towards my bedroom. "There is no shower, but let's get you washed and changed. Martin, make Daisy a mug of tea please, and bring into the bedroom."

The room had stopped swaying. I was clean and in comfortable jeans and sweatshirt. The tea that Martin had brought, passing it through a crack in the door, was drunk. "I feel better now. Thank you Maggie. I don't know what happened to me."

Tenby's voice came through the door. "Does Daisy need the doctor?" I shook my head at Maggie. She went to the door and replied, "no, she's much better now. She will be fine, after a meal and a good rest."

"I need a statement from her, I can take it later if she'd rather," said Tenby. I was sitting facing my dressing table mirror. They thought I couldn't see them. Tenby lent forward and kissed Maggie on the cheek. She smiled up at him and raised her hand to his cheek, giving it a little pat before she turned away. That's how it was, I thought. I had suspected for a long time, but now I had the evidence before me. I was delighted and was certain that they would find happiness together.

"I can give you my statement now," I told Tenby and followed him into the lounge. It was back to its normal state. Martin and Gerald I realised had been busy. They had removed all signs of Nigel's occupation, and Martin was loading the dishwasher with the last of Nigel's crockery, and the disgusting pizza plate. The sofa was occupied, one end of it. Three faces stared at me with a mixture of defiance and apprehension. Lottie was in the middle between Cleo and Flora. I was aware of Maggie and Tenby looking at the sofa, the animals, and then at me. I walked over to the sofa and looked down at the trio. "Okay. Lottie can stay, but no more befriending animals to bring into my cottage. And you all have to behave!" Lottie looked up at me, and I will swear that she gave me a grin. A large sigh of contentment came from her, and she put her head down on her paws, and went to sleep. Cleo licked her face, turned round and round on the spot, and went to sleep. Flora looked at both of them, looked at Tenby and then me, and drifted off to sleep snuggled beside her friend Lottie..

"How's Sheila? Is she okay?" I asked.

Martin started to laugh. "She never stopped talking for ages, telling us all about it again and again. Her daughter took her off back to her apartment so that she could wind down and crash out there. Jim is helping sort out all the dogs with the vet. He rushed up to check them all out."

CHAPTER FORTY ONE

It was two days later. A large postcard had arrived that morning with the usual sunny beach scene. This time it said in large print See *you soon Babe!* and the single word underneath *Thanks!* Of course I knew who it was from. Sam the gunman had been sending me the odd postcard for some time, but I had never been given the 'Babe' title before. Oh well, I suppose it was a better name than the one he usually wrote. Obviously, Gerald had told him that I hadn't objected to his return to Cornwall. The postcard had arrived with a letter for me that morning at breakfast. Puzzled, I opened the letter to find a note from Nigel. There had been a dispute since the divorce when he had gone off with items of jewellery, admittedly that he had presented to me over the years, but they were still mine. They would be returned by registered post that day. He concluded the letter by saying he never wanted to see me again, and that he was still in agony with his damaged toe. When I read this out at breakfast time, there was a chorus of approval, and the hope that it would continue to pain him.

Lisa and Jake had been to the cottage. Jake rang afterwards. "The garden is completely overgrown, with Ivy and Virginia creeper running riot up the walls. Mum, it's such a shame, there are some unusual plants overwhelmed by weeds. The house itself is just shabby and out of date. The bathroom and the kitchen need replacing, but it's a beautiful place. Yesterday afternoon when we looked over it, the sun flooded in the windows, making it welcoming and cheerful despite the shabby old furniture. We can live in the cottage quite happily for now. It will give us a chance to see how we like it, and what we will need to do to fix it. Most of the rooms will only need fresh paint. Lisa started crying when we walked out into the garden, she was just so grateful to find ourselves in possession of such a wonderful place. It's difficult to know what to say to grandmother, but when Lisa and I go tomorrow to visit her we can thank her properly then. We went up to the Holy Well chapel through the churchyard and along the fields. It's a beautiful place so peaceful. Lisa lit a candle and put it on the altar. We felt that we belonged in this village and our visit to the chapel reinforced that."

So much had happened since I had gone to greet my mother with Jake. Discovering the puppy farm, shooting the bad guy and my husband had been major highlights. The reaction the following day from our escape had been terrible. At points during that day I couldn't stop shaking. The stress that I had bottled up whilst coping with the ongoing situation seemed to flood my whole being. Not so Sheila! She was still telling everybody all about it! Sheila had only one regret. She hadn't been able to get to the gun before me and shoot somebody!

All the dogs and puppies were to be re-homed. It was a relief to see them go, not only would they have new homes, but I was very relieved that they would go to other homes, not mine! Lottie had been determined to make a home with Flora and Cleo in my cottage. She had her wish, and I had to admit she was no bother. Watching and following Flora around, she soon picked up the household rules. Her thin tiny tail wagged constantly, and the tiny claws clattered up and down the tiled floor after her companions.

Work had begun on the disused stable that was to become Gerald's new home. Next door to that Martin was organizing a gym, but the last stable he was keeping available for storage and Sheila's mobility scooter.

That afternoon the rain swept across Bodmin Moor, so heavy and spiteful that not one of us ventured out. The library, with its huge log fire, comfortable chairs and long windows, showed us the full extent of the storm, behind the rain spattered glass. Gerald and Martin had adjourned to the table with the maps they had used to find the puppy farm. Now, their new search was to be for archaeological remains. Jim, interested at first had reverted to his in-depth study of the Knights Templars in the area. The maps he had on his desk, were similar, but of a different age. Sheila was denying tiredness of any description, and had seated herself in her usual comfortable chair, complete with her knitting.

"Oh dear, isn't this boring? Nothing ever happens here, does it?" The words spoken quietly from her, caused everyone to jump and stare at Sheila in disbelief.

"Nothing ever happens! I would've thought that you would be glad of some peace and quiet after your experiences this week." Jim said.

I grinned, that was Sheila. If ever anyone loved life, it was Sheila.

Tenby strode into the library with a smile on his face. "Daisy and Sheila, we now know what is behind that locked door in the cavern." Satisfied that he had got everyone's full attention Tenby looked around at each and every one of us. His smile could not have been broader, as it was, it nearly split his face. "We found the proceeds of several country house burglaries." He waited until our exclamations had died down. "The villains were storing them behind that locked door. When the fuss had died down, they were then selling them, and some were even being transported to Europe. From what we have been told, the puppy farm was too much work and not enough profit. They thought they had found a vein of gold and started mining, but again that was far too much work for them. They didn't know how to proceed with the mine or offload the ore onto the market. Straightforward burglary was an easier option. You gave us a nasty scare Daisy and Sheila, and you're lucky to get out alive.

They were vicious thugs."

Martin spoke up from behind a book, "I have been approached to ask if I would like to buy Hilltop Farm and add it to the Priory land. I have agreed because I don't want any more trouble with that area of the moor, and I think that the cave should be in my hands."

"Great idea Martin. That way you can ensure that the property is used in keeping with the rest of the farms in the area," said Jim.

Life settled back into a routine, and if like Sheila, we all found it dull, not one of us said so.

"Sheila, you'll just have to get used to a quiet life," said Jim. "After all, it's not every day dead bodies arrive for us to investigate."

That's what he thought!

About Janey Clarke

Scottish born, I now live on the Jurassic coast of Dorset with my husband, and Monty our enormous Cavalier. Our two adult children live in Yorkshire and Germany.

As a lifelong sufferer from E.D.S, I cope with my restricted mobility by reading and writing. I often scribbled stories from childhood, stemming from Scotland, Cornwall, Norfolk, Essex, and the Home Counties.

Now a teacher, tutor, and hotelier, I still scribble with each novel disappearing into a drawer!

Changing primary schools, five in total, meant that I was unable to read until given special lessons. This gave me a deep love of reading, and being an only child, I devoured books. Following this experience, when I became unable to teach because of mobility problems, I became a home tutor. After extra training, I specialised in children with reading difficulties.

Still an avid reader, I love cosy mysteries, where the murder doesn't scare me to death! The Open University helped with my exams, enabling me to continue studying. I had an amanuensis who wrote out my answers. Of course, I did English and history, my great loves. Creative Writing was difficult as I love to write amusing and light pieces, and they preferred dark and dismal topics!

I studied botanical art for many years, and then got RSI. Determined to carry on with my art and writing, I now paint with my left hand and dictate all my novels. I still paint flowers trying to capture their beauty, it is hard work but so enjoyable.

Also By Janey Clarke

Daisy And The Deadly Dagger

www.blossomspringpublishing.com

Printed in Great Britain
by Amazon

79464908R10154